Of Magic and Mangers

Christmas Stories about The Story

By
Gene Wilder

Of Magic and Mangers: Christmas Stories about The Story
By Gene Wilder
Copyright © 2014 by Gene Wilder
Cover illustration and design by Lee Heidel, Heideldesign
Cover photograph by iStockphoto/ginosphotos
Author photograph by Ginger Heidel, Heideldesign
The Magic Which Makes the Difference first appeared in the Winter, 1997 issue of *E Street*.
So Let Your Light Shine, is based, in part, on a story written by Brett Younger entitled, "Someone left the lights on, and I'm just trying to jog past them," which first appeared in his book, *The Lighter Side* © 2012 by Nurturing Faith Inc.

The Light That Darkness Could Not Extinguish is a fictional account based on a similar event that took place in 1993, in Billings, Montana.

Published in the United States by **Create**space, an Amazon company
ISBN: 1495437973
ISBN-13: 9781495437977
LCCN: 2014906021
Notice of Rights
All rights reserved. No part of this book may be reproduced or transmitted in any form by any means, electronic, mechanical, photocopying, recording or otherwise, without the prior written permission of the author. For more information on getting permission for reprints or excerpts contact the author at gene@gene-wilder.com
Notice of Liability
This book is a work of fiction and a product of the author's imagination. Names, characters, places, and incidents are used fictitiously. Any resemblance to actual events, locales, or person, living or dead, is coincidental. While every precaution has been taken in the preparation of the book, neither the author, nor **Create**space, shall have any liability to any person or entity with respect to any loss or damage caused or alleged to be caused directly or indirectly by the contents of this book.

*To my dear wife, Pat.
The one who makes all my stories,
stories filled with love.*

Contents

Acknowledgements	vii
Preface	ix
Chapter 1: The Magic That Makes the Difference	1
Chapter 2: Christmas Tree or Christmas Treason?	10
Chapter 3: Egg Cartons and Mangers	18
Chapter 4: Home for Christmas	23
Chapter 5: But As Many as Received Him . . .	30
Chapter 6: O Little Town of Jefferson	39
Chapter 7: In Search of the Missing Christ Child	47
Chapter 8: The Real Reason for the Season	52
Chapter 9: The Bell Ringer's Friend	60
Chapter 10: It Came Upon a Midnight Drear	68
Chapter 11: The Night Christmas Came to Habeeb	76
Chapter 12: So Let Your Light Shine	84
Chapter 13: The Gift of a Homeless Man	94
Chapter 14: *Nunca Solo*	102
Chapter 15: The Light that Darkness Could Not Extinguish	113
About the Author	123

Acknowledgements

Storytellers are no better than the audiences to whom they tell their tale. That's why I must begin by acknowledging those who first heard my stories and encouraged me to write more. I owe a debt of gratitude to the members of West Highland Baptist Church in Macon, Georgia; First Baptist Church of Fitzgerald, Georgia; and First Baptist Church of Jefferson City, Tennessee. These dear friends not only affirmed me, but convinced me that my stories needed the larger audience afforded by the publication of a book.

Without the loving support of my daughter, Ginger Heidel; my son-in-law, Lee Heidel; and my granddaughter, Camille Heidel, this work probably would have remained nothing more than an idea. Two years ago when, as a Christmas gift, they gave me a professionally-collated version of my Christmas stories, they unleashed a dream that has now become a reality. Additionally, through their company, Heideldesign, they produced a book cover that is inviting, and an author's photo that helped me put my "best face" forward.

The encouragement and critique I received from the staff at **Create**Space have been invaluable, especially since this is my first attempt at publishing an entire book. The services they provided in both editing and layout helped produce a book I can market with confidence and pride.

Every author should be lucky enough to have an English teacher like Tanya Turner to proofread the text. I cannot begin to thank her enough for the countless hours she spent discovering those mistakes others would have missed.

On the back cover of this book, you will find quotes from Randall O'Brien and Tim Anderson. Both of these men are some of the brightest people I know. When I asked them to review my work and provide promotional critique, I was humbled by their graciousness. Their willingness to attach their names to my work is worth more to me than my words can express.

Last of all, I thank my dear wife, Pat. No encouragement has been more meaningful than hers. No proofreader has been more honest. No wife more supportive. While I bathed the words of this book with all the creativity I could muster, she bathed them with understanding and love. Without a doubt, this work has been a team effort, and she has been the star of the team.

Perhaps it goes without saying (but I must say it anyway), I am eternally thankful to the main character of this book, to the God who loved us enough to come in human form, to the Christ who gives ultimate meaning to any story about His story.

Preface

Few words engage the heart more quickly and completely than the words of a well-crafted story, and few stories are more engaging than the story of Christ's miraculous birth. But when it comes to the Christmas story, how can one retell it in a way that allows its hearers to catch it with fresh ears, to hear it as if hearing it for the very first time?

To preach fresh and engaging sermons during the Christmas season is the daunting task that faces all of us who make our living behind the pulpit. How do you say something fresh and engaging when almost everyone in your congregation knows the story by heart? And though the story itself is filled with wonder and awe, what can you say to keep familiarity from robbing the story of its magic and mystery?

Several years ago, when I was searching for a way to rekindle the magic of the Christmas story, I chose to write a Christmas sermon that was a story about the Christmas story. Not only did the "story sermon" become an immediate hit with adults and children alike, but it reinforced the meaning of the original story in fresh, new ways.

After that first year, as Christmas approached, members of my congregation began asking if another story sermon was forthcoming. Soon, I began to make it my practice to preach a Christmas story sermon every year on the Sunday before Christmas. These stories became my Christmas present to the members of my congregation.

The following chapters are edited versions of stories I have shared with my congregations. The central themes of the original Christmas story - hope, peace, joy, and love - come to life when woven through contemporary stories about the age-old biblical story. When the characters around the manger become as real as your next door neighbors, they begin to leap from the page and speak in a voice that is fresh and alive.

As you read my stories about the story, perhaps you will see yourself in some of my fictional characters, or you may find your town or your church nestled in one of my fictional locations. If you do, don't be surprised if the old story becomes *your* new story, a story filled with mystery and magic about the newborn babe, born in Bethlehem's manger.

one

The Magic That Makes the Difference

Dear friends, let us love one another, for love comes from God. Everyone who loves has been born of God and knows God. Whoever does not love does not know God, because God is love. This is how God showed his love among us: He sent his one and only Son into the world that we might live through him. This is love: not that we loved God, but that he loved us and sent his Son. . .

(1 John 4:7-10 NIV)

Timmy Edwards was near exhaustion as he looked into the cardboard carton and saw one last box of Christmas cards. All afternoon he had trudged from house to house selling cards to friends and neighbors. The cards were part of a fund-raising project for his fifth-grade class. They were raising money for the spring trip to Washington, D.C.

As he looked at that one last box, he tried to think of someone who might buy it. Over the last few hours, he had gone to every house on the street and had run out of potential buyers. Then he saw the unkempt house at the end of the street and wondered if he should approach Mr. Wadley.

Jim Wadley was rarely seen in public, and on those few occasions when he ventured out of his tattered old house, he shuffled along the less traveled backstreets like some frightened animal fearful of human contact. His hunched form betrayed the shadow of a man weighed down by something dark and heavy, burdened by some loathsome affliction he could hardly bear. Though the children dubbed him "The Meanest Man in Town," few really knew much about him, except that he lived alone with a dog named Smut, an old mutt who was part Chow and part Rottweiler.

Timmy felt a cold chill run up his spine as he looked toward the old Wadley house. Then, with a burst of courage, he said out loud, "It's almost Christmas. Surely Mr. Wadley can't be as mean as they say."

Night had begun to fall as Timmy walked up the sidewalk to Mr. Wadley's house. In the dim shadows, the house looked more sinister than it had earlier in the day. As the winter winds blew, the old, barren trees swayed back and forth, bending low to the ground like bony hands reaching out to grab whoever came near.

As Timmy approached the house, he saw one light shining in a back room. The rest of the house seemed cold, dark, and deserted. After taking a deep breath, Timmy walked to the door and knocked. Instantly, Smut started barking and growling and, within seconds, Timmy could hear him pawing at the front door. As the dog kept barking and growling, Timmy heard footsteps – slow, heavy footsteps – and for a second he thought about running away. But just then, the door opened as Mr. Wadley snarled, "What do you want, you pesky, little kid?"

Almost in a whimper, Timmy replied, "Ah . . . Mr. Wadley, . . . I'm selling Christmas cards for our fifth-grade class. I have one box left. Would you like to buy it?"

"Christmas cards," barked Wadley. "I don't believe in Christmas and, if I did, I certainly wouldn't be buying cards from some snotty-nosed kid like you. Now get out of here before I let my dog loose on you. Get out of here. I mean it. Get out of here now!"

Wadley needed to say no more. Timmy grabbed his carton of cards and began running for the road. Just as he did, Smut jerked away from his owner's grasp and began chasing the boy. Without warning, the dog lunged at Timmy, sinking its teeth into the back of his leg. As Timmy fell, Mr. Wadley grabbed the dog and pulled him back. When he did, Timmy got up and started running as hard as he could, not stopping until he finally reached his house.

After examining his injury, Timmy's parents took him to Doctor Sanders, their family physician, who promptly stitched him up and gave him a tetanus shot.

"Floyd," announced Doc Sanders, "I'm afraid we're going to have to put an end to Wadley's old dog. You know this isn't the first child he's bitten."

"I'm afraid you're right," admitted Timmy's father. "I'll call one of my deputies and have him go over to Wadley's place and pick up that old mutt tonight."

Floyd Edwards, Timmy's father, was the town sheriff, and in Donner's Glen the sheriff was in charge of animal control. As he picked up the phone to call the station, Doc Sanders interrupted, "Sheriff, you tell your boys not to damage the dog. We've got to keep him penned up for ten days to be sure he doesn't show signs of rabies."

"Ten days. I understand," said Floyd as he picked up the phone to make the call.

The next day was Sunday, and as they did every Sunday, Timmy and his family went to church. Timmy liked a lot of things about church, but he liked the children's sermon best. Rev. Jackson was inventive and always found some special way to make the Bible interesting.

On that Sunday, Rev. Jackson started the children's sermon by showing them a long, thin rod, covered in glitter. Then he asked, "Has anybody ever seen a magic wand?" Some of the little kids said they had, but Timmy was old enough to know that magic wands were just make-believe.

The pastor continued, "Suppose I had a magic wand that could turn bad things into good things. What would you want me to change?"

One of the kids said, "I'd like you to make my cavities go away."

"I'd like you to make bees that couldn't sting," replied one of the first graders.

"I'd like you to do away with homework," replied one of the older children as the adult members of the congregation began laughing.

Then, without even thinking, Timmy spoke up. "I'd like you to do some kind of magic to dogs so they wouldn't be mean and bite."

After fielding a few other responses, Rev. Jackson said, "A long time ago, God looked at the world and saw many things that needed to be different. He saw families that didn't care about each other. He saw people who would kill and steal. He saw people who told lies, people who cheated, and people who treated others in hateful, mean ways. As he looked down to the Earth, God asked himself, 'What kind of magic can I send to Earth that will really make a difference?" Finally, he decided the best magic he could send would be the magic of love. He knew that if people were touched by love, love would change them. Love would turn bad people into good people and mean people into nice people.

"To teach people how to love, God sent his son, Jesus. God knew that if people watched and listened to Jesus, they would learn how to love each other. And when they learned about love, love would be the magic that would make a difference.

"So you see, boys and girls, when we celebrate Christmas we are celebrating God's gift of love. Christmas is a celebration of God sending his magic, his magic called love. Because love is the magic that really makes a difference."

As Timmy left church that day, he thought about Rev. Jackson's sermon. He wondered if love really was the magic that could make a difference. Would mean people really become nice people if you gave them enough love? Would people who hurt others really be changed if somebody returned that hurt with love? Was love really the magic that makes a difference?

―⁂―

Later that afternoon, Timmy and his friend Jason rode their bikes down to the vet's office so Timmy could show Jason the dog that had bitten him. As they pulled into the parking lot behind the vet's office, Timmy could see the holding pens. Several dogs were in the pens, and when the dogs saw the boys on their bikes, they all started barking at once.

But one bark seemed different than the others. It was that ugly growl of old Smut. Even though Timmy knew Smut couldn't get out, that terrible growl almost made him sick. This was the meanest dog in town, owned by the meanest man in town. "What a pair," Timmy said to himself as old Smut began to show his teeth.

—⁂—

That night, Timmy and his family began decorating their house for Christmas. As Timmy's sister finished decorating the tree, Timmy set up the nativity scene. For several minutes he adjusted and readjusted the figurines. Finally, when all the other characters seemed to be in the right place, he put baby Jesus in the manger. As he did, he remembered the words of Rev. Jackson, "God sent Jesus to teach us how to love, because love is the magic that makes a difference."

When Timmy went to bed that night he couldn't stop thinking about Mr. Wadley and his mean dog. Mr. Wadley was one of the meanest people he had ever met, and his dog was just like him. Again, he remembered what Rev. Jackson had said about love. He said, "If people were touched by love, love would change them. Love would turn bad people into good people and mean people into nice people." Timmy wondered if the magic of love would work on Mr. Wadley and Smut.

—⁂—

The next morning at breakfast, Timmy asked, "Dad, why do you think Mr. Wadley is so mean?"

After stirring his cup of coffee, the sheriff responded, "Jim Wadley has not always been like he is now, son. In fact, Jim was one of my best friends as we were growing up. We played football together, and on several occasions we even went on camping trips together.

"Jim was also a very talented singer. Our church used to have a big, Christmas pageant every year, and Jim Wadley was always the featured soloist. Hundreds of people came to church mainly to hear Jim sing, 'Sweet Little Jesus Boy.' No one could sing it better."

"But Dad," interrupted Timmy, "when Mr. Wadley yelled at me, he told me he didn't believe in Christmas."

"Well, you see, son, something happened on Christmas Eve about ten years ago, something that changed Jim Wadley. It happened right after the Christmas Eve service. Jim had been to the Christmas Eve service with his wife and son. As they were traveling home, a drunk driver ran into their car. Jim was seriously hurt. It took him months to recover from his injuries. His wife and son were killed, an injury from which Jim has never recovered. Ever since that accident, Jim has never been the same. He stays up in that old house with his dog and seldom has anything to do with the rest of the folks in this town."

—m—

That afternoon, Timmy again rode by the vet's. This time he brought along some dog biscuits. As he walked toward old Smut's pen, he again heard the growl that scared him two nights earlier. Smut looked so mean, with his face snarled and his teeth showing. Again, Timmy felt the urge to run away, but he fought back the fear and walked a little closer. When he got about five or six steps from the pen, he reached in his pocket, pulled out a dog biscuit, and threw it into Smut's pen. At first, the dog ignored the biscuit, continuing to growl as before; but finally he stopped growling and ate the biscuit. When he finished, Timmy threw him another, and then a third one. Finally Smut stopped growling altogether and just chewed away on the doggy treats.

Over the next week, Timmy continued to take dog treats to the dog pen. Instead of growling whenever Timmy rode up, Smut would bark with excitement and happily wag his tail. Each day, Timmy would walk a little closer to the pen until he finally got close enough to pet Smut on the head. In return, Smut licked Timmy's hand as though the two had been life-long friends.

Timmy got up early on Christmas Eve morning, excited about going to the vet's to see old Smut. He had a special treat for him, an old ham bone left over from last night's supper. After eating his breakfast, Timmy slipped on his jacket and started out the door.

As he did, his father spoke, "Timmy, before you leave, I wanted to tell you the good news. You won't have to worry about getting rabies shots. It's been ten days since Smut bit you, and he shows no signs of disease. One thing's for sure, after today that dog won't be biting anybody else."

"What do you mean?" asked Timmy.

"I mean they'll be putting Smut to sleep this afternoon, so you won't have to worry about him again."

"But Daddy," Timmy protested. "Smut's not such a bad dog. All he needed was some love. Love has made Smut a different dog. Please don't let anything happen to him. I know he won't bite again."

Over the next few minutes, Timmy and his father continued to argue about Smut, but to no avail. Smut had bitten twice and nothing would change the sheriff's mind.

When Timmy's dad left for work, Timmy headed straight for the vet's. As soon as he rode up, Smut began wagging his tail and barking excitedly. When Timmy pulled the ham bone out of his pocket, Smut jumped up on the fence with all the excitement of a younger pup.

"I won't let anything happen to you," assured Timmy as he reached through the fence, stroking Smut's head. You're not a bad dog. You're not a bad dog at all. You're just a dog that needed the magic of love."

All morning long, Timmy sat by the pen playing with Smut. Around eleven o'clock, the vet walked out to the pen.

"Watch yourself, Timmy," called out the vet. "That dog has bitten before, and he might bite again."

"No, he won't," Timmy cried out. "He's a different dog than he used to be. He's a dog that has been changed by the magic of love. Please don't put him to sleep. Old Smut won't hurt anybody again. Please. Please don't put him to sleep."

"Timmy, I don't have a choice," replied the vet. "Your father's the sheriff and he's in charge of these things. He's the only one who can keep Smut alive. Unless you can change his mind, I'll have to put Smut to sleep."

Just then, Timmy's dad drove up, and Timmy went running to the car. "Dad, Dad, please tell the vet not to kill Smut. He's not a mean dog. He's the nicest dog I've ever seen. He won't hurt anybody. Just watch."

Even as he was pleading, Timmy ran over, opened the gate, and got in the pen with Smut. Immediately, the dog jumped up and started licking Timmy on the face. When Timmy's father saw the bond of love that tied his son and the dog, he knew he couldn't put Smut to sleep. Doing so would break his son's heart.

Finally, he spoke, "OK, Timmy. Smut can live, but we'll have to take him back to his owner. He's not your dog. He belongs to Mr. Wadley. And let me warn you, if that dog ever bites anyone else, there will be no third chance for Old Smut."

Night had begun to fall as Timmy walked up the sidewalk to Mr. Wadley's house. When he knocked on the door, he shivered as he heard the same heavy footsteps he had heard ten days before.

"Who is it?" barked Wadley from behind the closed door.

"It's Timmy Edwards, the boy who was bitten by your dog. Please let me in."

"Go away," growled Wadley. "I don't have that dog anymore. So go away and leave me alone."

"But Mr. Wadley, I have a Christmas present for you. Please let me in."

As Timmy spoke, Mr. Wadley cracked open the door just enough to peek outside. When he did Smut stuck his nose though the open door and pushed his way inside. Once inside, he jumped up on Mr. Wadley, licking him from head to toe.

"Merry Christmas, Mr. Wadley. Merry Christmas from me and Smut."

As Wadley looked at the dog, then at the boy, tears began streaming down his cheeks. Then without warning, Jim Wadley reached out and began hugging the boy. He hugged him for the longest time, thanking him for all he had done.

As Timmy walked back to the car, he heard a sound coming from inside the house. It was the sound of singing. It was a beautiful voice singing the loveliest song he had ever heard.

Sweet little Jesus boy. You must-a been born in a manger.
Oh, sweet little holy chil', they didn't know who you was.

As Timmy got into his parents' car, his father reached around and gave him the biggest hug. "Timmy, it's been ten years since I've heard Mr. Wadley sing. You did something tonight I thought was impossible."

"Oh, Dad, nothing's impossible," replied Timmy. "Nothing's impossible if you use the Christmas magic – the magic that God sent to us in his Son Jesus. Nothing's impossible with the magic of love."

two

Christmas Tree or Christmas Treason?

Get rid of all bitterness, rage and anger, brawling and slander, along with every form of malice. Be kind and compassionate to one another, forgiving each other, just as in Christ God forgave you.
(Ephesians 4:31-32 NIV)

As Martha Boswell looked into her husband's weary face, she could tell he was not a happy camper. The stress lines etched across his forehead were exclamation marks, and the angry twist of his mouth looked like some kind of emotional misprint. As he walked into the kitchen and began to pour his first cup of coffee, she braced herself for the explosion she knew would come. She did not have to wait long.

"That's the last straw," barked George Boswell, as he vigorously stirred his coffee. "I've always considered myself a patient man, but those inconsiderate neighbors have finally pushed me to the breaking point. Their pigheaded stubbornness will not cost me another night's sleep! If the Greshams think I'm gonna ignore this last insult, they've got another thing coming."

The Greshams and Boswells had lived beside each other for over twenty-eight years. The two families had moved into their houses within a week of each other. As young newly-weds, both families were just getting started. George Boswell had just taken over his father's plumbing business, and Mark Gresham had gotten his first job as an accountant with a small firm on the other side of town. Martha Boswell and Ellen Gresham were both teachers. Ellen taught English at Concord High, and Martha was a kindergarten teacher at a private school in Grayton.

The Gresham's two children, Cindy and Mark, Jr., were born within months of the Boswells' two children, Anne and Eddie. Throughout the years, the four children had been inseparable. Quite often, the four were mistaken for brothers and sisters instead of next door neighbors.

Until five years ago, the Boswells and Greshams did everything together. They went on vacation together, shared holidays together, and even considered investing in joint ownership of a cabin in the mountains. Yes, up until five years ago, the Boswells and Greshams were joined at the heart, but in the last half decade, the two families had not shared a word.

As George Boswell sat down at the breakfast table, Martha asked, "George, what are you gonna do?"

"I'm not sure," he replied, while crunching on a spoon-full of cornflakes. "I'll probably call Jake Dinsmore's office and see what legal recourse I've got. Or I just might go to Sears, buy a chainsaw, and cut the tree down myself. One thing for sure, when the sun sets tonight, those stupid blinking lights won't be shining in my bedroom window."

"George, you can't cut that pine tree down," cautioned Martha. "It's squarely on the property line. You cut that tree down and the Greshams will take us to court."

"Well, let 'em take us to court," barked George. "There's bound to be a law against keeping your neighbor up all night with the lights of a blinking Christmas tree just outside his bedroom window."

As Martha thought about the contention that surrounded the tree, she couldn't help remembering when it was first planted. The large pine was twenty-seven years old. George and Mark had planted it the first Christmas after moving into their houses. She almost laughed as she remembered them taking such great pains to string a line between the surveyor's property markers. Both men looked like little boys who had just pricked their fingers so that they could become blood brothers. They were intent on making sure the tree was right in the middle of the property line. This tree was to be a sign of a friendship to last forever. Now it was the most recent episode in the families' five-year feud.

As the secretary unlocked the office door, she could hear the phone ringing. Quickly, she yanked up the receiver and caught her breath as she said, "Dinsmore, Franklin and Cline."

"Yeah, this is George Boswell. I need to talk with Jake Dinsmore."

"I'm sorry, sir," replied Jake's secretary in a voice that betrayed no sorrow at all. "Mr. Dinsmore is out of the office and will not return until after the holidays. Can I take a message and ask him to call you when he returns?"

"No, that'll be too late," barked George in a voice loud enough to distort over the phone receiver. "I haven't slept all night. I need to talk to him today. I guess I'll have to call him at home."

"Sir, I'm afraid it won't do any good to call him at home. He's gone to Virginia to spend the holidays with family, and he left strict orders not to be disturbed until he returns."

"Well, what am I supposed to do while he's flitting across the country?" chided George. "Oh, just forget it," he finally replied in a voice of resignation. "Maybe I'll just buy a chainsaw instead."

Before the secretary could respond, George hung up.

As Martha looked out the kitchen window at the pine tree covered in Christmas lights, she started thinking about Christmases in the past when the two families decorated the tree together. Those were good days. In those early days, neither family had much money, nor did they need much to decorate the tree. It was so small that one string of outdoor lights was more than adequate.

As the tree grew, so did the families' incomes. Each year, the decorations became more and more elaborate until the pine on the line became the showpiece of the neighborhood.

The most distinctive decoration on the tree was a three foot angel perched on the tree top. Because the lights were so bright and the angel was so realistic-looking, people would come to their neighborhood just to get a look at the tree.

But over the last five years, the large angel stayed tucked away, collecting dust, in the Boswell's basement while the tree shivered dark in the winter wind, a tragic indicator of the darkness that engulfed their broken friendship.

Sadly, the pine that had once been the most beautiful Christmas tree in town had now become the tree of Christmas treason.

—⁂—

Martha's reminiscence was interrupted as she heard someone come in the front door. When she looked around the corner, she couldn't believe what she saw. George was standing there with a new chainsaw under his arm.

"George," exclaimed Martha in tones of disbelief, "I didn't really think you were serious about buying a chainsaw!"

"You bet I'm serious," he said. "I will not let those Christmas lights rob me of another night's sleep. If the Greshams don't take those lights down, then I'm taking the tree down."

Martha could tell he was serious, and though she had no desire to make the Greshams her friends, she didn't want their war of words to escalate into a Christmas chainsaw massacre.

"George," implored Martha, "you can't just go and cut down that tree. It's on the property line so it belongs to them as much as it does to us."

"Since I put it up, I guess I can take it down," retorted George.

"Please, George," pled Martha. "At least go over and talk to them before you start cutting on the tree. It probably won't do any good, but at least it will give you some leverage if they take you to court."

As much as George dreaded a face to face confrontation with the Greshams, he knew Martha was right. He was certain the Greshams had strung up the lights this year simply to irritate him and was equally certain that talking to them would accomplish nothing, but if he ended up in court, he needed to demonstrate that he had tried to be civil before cutting down the tree.

"All right," sighed George, "I'll give 'em one last chance to act like civil human beings, but if they won't listen to reason, I'm cutting the tree down." And with that, he left the house and strode across the yard headed for the Gresham's front door.

―⚏―

As George approached the house, he paused, remembering the harsh words exchanged the last time he stood at that front door. Since that day, five years ago, silence and a property line were the only things the two neighbors had shared.

Those last few words had been exchanged in the spring of 1998. They were words culminating a week of bitter arguing. It was the spring when Eddie was scheduled to graduate from Concord High. After graduation, he was promised a scholarship to UT to play football for the Tennessee Volunteers. No one was prouder than George.

Then came the bad news. It shouldn't have come as a surprise, but it did. All year long, Ellen had warned George and Martha about Eddie's English grades, but her warnings, for the most part, fell on deaf ears. Eddie had never been a model student and had always struggled with English, but George and Martha didn't worry about him failing, especially in his senior year, since his English teacher was their best friend and next door neighbor.

The news came a week before graduation. Eddie had been taken off the graduating list. Since he was failing English, there was no way he could graduate. Obviously, his dreams of playing football at UT vanished when his name disappeared from the graduation list.

At first, the two families tried to discuss the situation reasonably, but when it became obvious Eddie would fail, reasonable words quickly turned into angry accusations. As George now looked at the front steps, he remembered the last thing he said to Mark Gresham as he walked away.

"Hell will freeze over before I walk through these doors again."

George's troubled reflections were suddenly interrupted by the voice of a kind-looking lady dressed in nurse's scrubs.

"Hello, there," she said as she walked up the sidewalk. "I'm Florence Benson." I guess you're here to visit Mark."

Before George could answer, she continued. "Did you see the tree last night? Wasn't it beautiful? I'm so glad the Gresham children strung up the lights so that Mark could see them one last time."

"One last time? What do you mean?" asked George.

"Oh, excuse me for not properly introducing myself," said the lady. "I just assumed you knew I was their hospice nurse. I don't think I've met you. Are you a member of Mark's family?"

Startled, George wasn't sure how to respond. If a hospice nurse was coming to see Mark Gresham, that could mean only one thing. Mark was dying.

"Oh no," George replied, "I'm just one of Mark's neighbors. We both moved into this neighborhood about the same time."

"Well, I'm sure he'll appreciate your visit," she said. "But please don't stay too long. It takes all the energy he's got left to carry on the shortest conversation. I'm afraid, by this time next week, he may not be conscious at all. That's why I'm glad his kids put up the tree lights.

For some reason, putting lights on that old pine seemed to be Mark's final obsession. Last night when he looked at them from his bed, they seemed to give him a new sense of joy."

Without saying a word, George began to weep. In that single instant, all the stubbornness of five years weighed on him like snow weighs on a brittle limb just before it breaks. Not knowing what else to do, George turned and ran, retreating past the light-laden tree to the refuge of his home.

As he came through the front door and glanced at the new chainsaw, the pain of his grief was only surpassed by his guilt and his shame. His neighbor was dying, and he didn't even know it because he had let a war of words become a wall of wills between him and his life-long friend.

As night began to fall, Mark Gresham had difficulty distinguishing between reality and illusion. The drugs he was taking to manage his pain made it difficult to determine what was real. For several minutes, he twisted in bed to find a more comfortable position; then he turned toward the window so that he could look out at the tree. As his face turned toward the window, the brightly-colored lights mirrored off the surface of his pale, moist skin. His family took comfort in the warmth of his smile, thankful they had broken the five years of darkness by restringing the lights.

Then all of a sudden, Mark began to gasp. Quickly family members surrounded him, fearful of what this new symptom might mean.

"Is it real or am I hallucinating?" Mark shouted.

"What do you mean?" cried his daughter Cindy.

"Is the angel back on top of the tree or is it just a figment of my imagination?"

As the family members turned and looked out the window, they quickly saw what had captured Mark's attention. The pine tree was lighted, just as it had been the night before, but this time there was a new light. Nestled against the top of the tree was a bright, three-foot angel, a sign of friendship resurrected from the bottom of the Boswell's basement, a light of love resurrected from the depths of the Boswells' heart.

As the Gresham family stood there staring in awed disbelief, visitors entered the room. There, with tears streaming down their faces, stood Martha and George Boswell.

George spoke first. "You always told us that true neighbors never had to knock so we decided to let ourselves in."

Then in a voice that was warm but weak, Mark replied, "But wasn't it you, who said, 'Hell would freeze over before you walked through those doors again?'"

"Yes, that's what I said," replied George. "And I meant every word of it. So I guess that's why I'm here tonight. Hell froze over and now I'm here. I guess you could say that the fires of my hate were extinguished by the warmth of Christmas love."

―☽―

Over the next few hours, the two families wept together, laughed together and prayed together in a room that was bathed in the light of Christmas love. As the angel stood tall atop the old pine, there was no disagreement about the tree. This, indeed, was a real Christmas tree. No longer was it a tree of Christmas treason. Once again it had become the tree of Christmas love.

three

Egg Cartons and Mangers

> *As Jesus looked up, he saw the rich putting their gifts into the temple treasury. He also saw a poor widow put in two very small copper coins. "Truly I tell you," he said, "this poor widow has put in more than all the others. All these people gave their gifts out of their wealth; but she out of her poverty put in all she had to live on."*
> *(Luke 21:1-4 NIV)*

As I climbed into the attic to get our Christmas decorations, my eye caught the box labeled, "Christmas Stuff from Mom and Dad's." The contents of the box were infused with warm memories of the Christmases I celebrated as a child. Each year those old, worn ornaments and antiquated lights reminded me of good times from the past, times when my parents were living, times when they always found a way to make Christmases special despite their meager incomes. Because the ornaments had become so brittle and fragile, rarely did I remove them from the box. Instead, I cuddled each piece with care as my mind idly wandered down memory lane.

When I opened the box and rummaged through its treasure, my mind was flooded by memories of Christmases past. Lying at the top of the box were those huge, hand-painted tree ornaments. Though the paint and glitter had begun to chip off, I still considered them to be some of the most beautiful ornaments I'd ever seen. At one time the box held a dozen ornaments, but several had slipped through excited children's hands so only seven survived.

Next, I saw the sleigh bells. Most of them were still connected to the red and green cloth straps. As I pulled them out, they began to jingle, and I remembered that Christmas when I had tied them to Sparky, the family dog. I thought Sparky would make a good reindeer, but for reasons known only to him, Sparkly was an unwilling participant. I still remember how he ran around in circles and rolled on the floor until he was finally free of his festive harness.

As I dug deeper in the box, I came across my favorite set of tree lights. They were unlike any I had seen before or since. Each light was a glass tube filled with colored water. When you plugged in the lights, the colored water bubbled as if it were slowly boiling. As a boy, I can remember watching for hours as the bubbles ascended through the glowing, colored liquid.

The item at the bottom of the box had been a mystery for years. It was obviously homemade and not very pretty. It was an old egg carton covered with patches of glitter. When I picked it up, I vaguely remembered seeing it as a child, and in the recesses of my memory, I sensed it had some kind of special meaning, but its meaning had faded with time.

Looking at it more closely, I could faintly make out a few words scribbled on the top of the carton in pencil. The message said, "Merry Christmas, Brother Mack, from Myrtle Mullins."

Myrtle Mullins. The name sounded familiar. And while I didn't quickly remember the name Myrtle, I remembered some Mullins kids I used to play with as a child.

All the folks who lived in my neighborhood were poor, but the Mullins family might have been the poorest family in town. Sometimes I saw them at school wearing shoes with large gaping holes, and while the rest of us would bring sandwiches and cookies for lunch, the Mullins children would sometimes have nothing more than a piece of old stale cornbread. I couldn't remember for sure, but I thought their mother's name might have been Myrtle.

Each year, I thought about throwing away the old egg carton, but since my parents had kept it, I assumed it must have some kind of significance. So instead of discarding it, I kept tucking it away in the bottom of the box.

I'm not sure why, but something within my heart convinced me to bring the egg carton out of its hiding, to once again let it be part of our family's Christmas celebration. So without fanfare, I took it downstairs with the rest of the decorations and set it under the tree until I could find a place where it was better suited.

The next day, my cousin Ron stopped by for a visit. Though he was four years older, we often played together as boys. When he looked at the tree, the first thing that caught his eye was the bubbling Christmas lights.

"You know Gene," he began, "I think your family had the only set of those bubbling Christmas lights I've ever seen. When we were kids, I can remember watching those lights for hours."

As Ron was looking at the lights, he caught sight of the glittered egg carton. "I see you kept Old Widow Mullins egg carton, didn't you?"

Quickly, Ron's recognition got my attention.

"You mean you know the story behind this old, glittered box?" I asked.

"I sure do," replied Ron. "I was standing on the porch when Widow Mullins brought it to your father. Back then, I thought it was a silly present, but now it doesn't seem so silly anymore."

"Was there anything in the carton?" I asked, enthralled with curiosity.

"Eleven eggs," my cousin said. "Yes, Old Widow Mullins brought your dad eleven eggs.

"Don't you remember, when we were growing up, your dad was one of the few people in our community who owned a car. Being a country preacher, he used the car to take poor people to the doctor, the hospital, or wherever they needed to go.

"Mrs. Mullins was a widow lady who lived down the road. She was very poor and often sick. Everything she owned was 'hand-me-downs.'

I remember feeling sorry for her one day when she came to your house and asked your dad for help. I could sense her embarrassment as she said, 'Brother Mack, I hate to be a burden again, but I need to go to the doctor and I don't have no money.' Of course, your father assured her she was no burden and gladly took her to the doctor's office.

"One Christmas Eve, when we were here for a visit, I was on the front porch as Mrs. Mullins came walking up to the house. In her hand she carried that cardboard egg carton, covered in glitter. As she got to the house, your father met her with a smile and asked, 'Ms. Mullins, what can I do for you today? Do you need a ride into town?'

"Nope,' she responded. 'I jis come up here to give you these eggs. My hens laid eleven this morning, so I decided to bring them all to you. I wisht I could of brung a dozen, but eleven is all the eggs I got. I just wanted to say Merry Christmas, Brother Mack, and to thank you for all the things you do.'"

After my cousin Ron left the house, I found myself staring at the old egg carton for the longest time. As I thought about the love that prompted the gift, I realized the old egg carton didn't look so ugly any more.

As I looked at that crude, glittered ornament, I thought about the Christmas story. The Christmas story was a lot like the egg carton. If you look at it without knowing the meaning, it's not very pretty at all. There's nothing pretty about a smelly, old barn with a muddy, dirt floor. There's nothing pretty about a crude, wooden hay trough or an old, cow pen. Dirty floors, smelly hay, and drafty barns are certainly not the settings one typically defines with the word "beautiful." Like an old egg carton, they are crude and ugly, unless you know the story.

Old Mrs. Mullins came on Christmas Eve because she loved my father. She loved him for all he had done to help her. When she came, she didn't bring much, not even a dozen eggs; but she gave my father the best she had, and because her gift was given in love, my father treasured it for the rest of his life.

On Christmas Eve, a long time ago, Jesus came to show us God's love. His coming didn't look like much: a poor Jewish babe, wrapped in hand-me-down clothes, tucked away in a feeding trough at the back of the barn. But today, you and I cherish that manger scene. We put it up for all to see because we know the story. We know that this crude and ugly scene is the beautiful story of God's love.

Yes, egg cartons and mangers take on a special beauty when you know that their story is the story of love.

four

Home for Christmas

And she brought forth her first-born son, and wrapped him in swaddling clothes and laid him in a manager; because there was no room for them in the inn.
(Luke 2:7 KJV)

The registered letter came. Josh knew it would, but knowing didn't soften the pain. As he read those precisely crafted terms of legalese, one word jumped out – FORECLOSURE. In thirty days the bank would take possession of the old home place. In thirty days Josh and his family would have no place to call their home.

Foreclosure notices never come at a good time, but this was the worst time. Josh and his family had to be out of the old home place by December 18, one week before Christmas. What a sad time to say goodbye to a house filled with so many Christmas memories.

—※—

Built in 1892, the old, two-story house had been the center of the Anderson's family Christmas celebration for over a century. Every year, at Christmas time, Anderson family members from all over the country came to the old home place to celebrate their love for each other and their love for Christ.

To be quite honest, it was Josh's memories of Christmas that motivated him to renovate the old place. Five years ago, when his father died, Josh inherited the old house, and though the place held a wealth of treasured memories, the house itself was hardly a treasure. Years of neglect left it needing considerable repair. Everything needed replacing. The plumbing, the wiring, the heating, and even the windows had seen better days. Many of those old, hand-hewn timbers had rotted, and no amount of patching seemed to stop the plaster from falling off the walls.

Josh thought about tearing down the old place but just couldn't do it. It held too many fond memories. Instead, he and Marie decided to renovate it. They realized it would be expensive, but since both of them had good jobs at the battery plant, they had no difficulty getting a loan.

One year later, the renovation was complete, and the old home place was as grand as ever. Granted, the renovation cost more than expected, but they knew they could make the mortgage payments if they were careful with their money.

The first year or so, they had no trouble with the payments. Of course, the birth of Janice and Jenny, their delightful twins, put a strain on their budget; but even with the babies, they were still getting by. At least they were until a year ago when the town's battery plant closed, and that's when their troubles began.

When the battery plant shut down, new jobs were almost impossible to find. Marie started cleaning houses and Josh picked up an odd job here and there, but their total family income just wasn't enough. For a month or so, they lived off their meager savings, but that soon ran out, forcing them to live on their slim earnings, their unemployment checks, and a monthly allotment of food stamps.

Now, with Christmas just days away, Josh Anderson faced the hard, cold facts. This year, there would be no Christmas celebration at the old home place. In fact, this year, the Andersons would not even have a place to call home.

Ann McLloyd really didn't need a housecleaner, but she hired Marie because she knew the Andersons needed the income. Every Monday and Thursday Marie would drive to the country and spend the bigger part of the day cleaning the McLloyds' large home.

On the first Monday after Thanksgiving, Marie showed up to clean the McLloyd's home as usual, but as she worked, Ann could tell something was wrong. Marie was strangely quiet and on several occasion Ann thought she saw her crying.

"Marie," began Ann, "I don't want to pry into your private affairs, but is something going on you need to talk about?"

At first, Marie said nothing; then, as the dam of her pent up emotions burst, a torrent of tears flooded her face.

"What is it?" asked Ann as she touched Marie's shoulder.

"Ann, the bank's foreclosing on the Old Anderson Home Place. We're going to lose it all. First we lost our jobs, then we lost our savings, and in two more weeks we're going to lose our home."

At first, Ann wasn't sure what to say so she just held Marie as she sobbed. She wanted to help, but wasn't sure what she could do.

Then she thought about their old barn. Several years ago, they had turned the loft of the old barn into a small apartment. Ann and her husband stayed there while workers renovated their own old house. Once the work on their house was finished, they moved out of the barn, and no one had lived there since.

"Marie," said Ann. "We have a place for your family to stay until you can get back on your feet."

"What do you mean?" asked Marie.

"Have you seen the old red barn that sits off the road as you drive up to our house?"

Marie nodded.

"Well, there's a small apartment in the loft. It's not very big, but you and your family are welcome to stay there as long as you want."

"We can't afford the rent," said Marie.

"Oh, no rent charged," said Ann with a reassuring smile. "The loft apartment's one of the benefits that comes with your job."

—⁂—

Until you've been evicted you really don't understand the embarrassment of losing your home. There's a shame that follows you like a dirge of disappointment, and it makes you feel little and ugly. Even good friends talk to you in a different tone. You can tell they want to say something helpful but just don't know what to say. Sometimes they avoid you so they don't have to say anything at all.

Josh and Marie faced double embarrassment. Not only did they have to face townsfolk, but they had to call every member of the Anderson family and explain why there would be no Christmas at the old home place - no Christmas this year, next year, or ever again - because the old home place was no longer their old home place. It was now repossessed property held by a mortgage lender.

When uncles, aunts, cousins, and nephews got the phone call, they all had the same reaction – shock and disbelief! Christmas at the old home place had been their life-long tradition. How could the Andersons celebrate Christmas if the old home place was gone?

Most family members tried to sound sympathetic, but Josh could hear the disappointment in their voices. With a few, he heard the tone of blame, and with each call he felt a growing burden of guilt and of shame.

—⁂—

The loft apartment was small, but cozy, and the Andersons were ever so grateful for the McLloyds' kindness. Moving from the old home place was hard, but once they said their goodbyes to the house, to the yard and to the old oak tree with the homemade swing, they determined to have the best Christmas they could, even if this year's celebration would be different.

Though there wasn't much room in the loft apartment, the family was able to squeeze a lighted tree in the corner of the living area and put some candles in the windows. It didn't look like the old home place, but it did look and smell like Christmas.

Up until the week before Christmas, Josh and Marie wondered where they'd find money to purchase gifts for the kids, but on the Sunday before Christmas, their worries were put to rest. On the way to Sunday School, Pastor Finley met Josh in the hall. After pulling him aside, he handed him an envelope that contained a gift card to Target.

"This was purchased by the members of the Dorcas Sunday School class," he said. "They know times are tough for you guys and wanted to help with Christmas. They especially want you to buy something nice for the twins."

It was hard for Josh to accept the gift, but sometimes pride gives way to necessity, and Josh realized, in a strange sort of way, that this was not just a gift. It was an act of God's grace.

In those last days before Christmas, Josh thought a lot about losing the old home place. As long as he could remember, the Anderson family always came to the old home place for Christmas. The place and the day seemed inseparable. The place and the day were all tied up together in one bright Christmas package, a package that the Andersons would never open again.

Despite their struggles, Marie and the twins were starting to feel better about Christmas. Granted, they weren't in the old home place, but at least they had a place and, through the generosity of the Dorcas class, they had gifts to share on Christmas.

As always, on Christmas Eve, the family bundled up and headed to their church's Christmas Eve service. The service was simple but always so meaningful. During the service they lit candles, sang carols, and heard the Christmas story read from the second chapter of Luke. The passage was so familiar that Josh could almost quote it by heart, but despite its familiarity, he always seemed to find something fresh and meaningful when he heard it again on Christmas Eve.

When the Christmas Eve service was over, the Andersons went back to their barn-loft apartment. After sharing a special meal they put Janice and Jenny to bed. Sleep did not come quickly for the twins. Only after several stern warnings about delaying the visit of Santa did the girls succumb to slumber.

Once the girls were asleep, Josh put on his coat and walked outside. He needed some time alone, some time to clear his head and to pick up the pieces of his broken heart.

So much had happened in the last year. His life had changed in ways he never imagined, and he wondered if Christmas would ever return to normal again.

As he walked away from the old barn, he looked across the pasture. It was a surreal scene, a quiet hillside shadowed by grazing cattle and snow-bent trees, all dimly lit by a half moon surrounded with the winter brilliance of stars. Out in the distance, he could see the form of cows and horses huddled around the old stable, feeding from hay left earlier in the day.

The view reminded him of one he'd seen earlier that evening. Shadowed trees looked like the dimly lit pews of the church and twinkling stars reminded him of the flickering flames of the candles. The cows at the stable reminded him of the nativity scene dimly lit at the altar.

As he took a deep breath of the cool, night air, he remembered those familiar words from the Gospel of Luke. Softly he whispered them, *And she brought forth her first-born son, and wrapped him in swaddling clothes and laid him in a manager; because there was no room for them in the inn.*

Quietly, the truth began to engulf him. Mary and Joseph didn't celebrate the birth of Christ at their old home place. They celebrated the first Christmas in – in a borrowed barn. For Mary and Joseph, the glory of Christmas had nothing to do with the place - but with the person. It had nothing to do with what they owned, but with whom they loved. Yes, the glory of the story was seen in the Christ, not in the barn.

And so it was for Josh, a homeless pilgrim celebrating Christmas in the shadow of a borrowed barn. The glory of Christmas had nothing to do with the place but with the person. The meaning of Christmas had nothing to do with what Josh owned, but with those he loved. Yes, the glory of this Christmas would be like the glory of the first Christmas, seen in the Christ, not in the barn!

No angels sang, and yet the strains of the old carol floated through the air with a meaning Josh had never grasped before:

Gentle Mary laid her child, lowly in a manger.
There He lay the undefiled, to the world a stranger.
Such a Babe in such a place, can he be the savior?
Ask the saved of all the race, who have found His favor.

And so that night, on Christmas Eve, Josh Anderson discovered the true glory of the Christmas story. The glory of the story was not found "in such a place." The glory of the story was found "in such a Savior."

five

But As Many as Received Him . . .

> *In the beginning was the Word, and the Word was with God, and the Word was God. The same was in the beginning with God. All things were made by him; and without him was not any thing made that was made. In him was life; and the life was the light of men. And the light shineth in darkness; and the darkness comprehended it not. . . That was the true Light, which lighteth every man that cometh into the world. He was in the world, and the world was made by him, and the world knew him not. He came unto his own, and his own received him not. But as many as received him, to them gave he power to become the sons of God, even to them that believe on his name . . .*
> *(John 1:1-5, 9-12 KJV)*

When the doorbell rang, Bobby Stone drowsily stirred from his fitful sleep and glanced at the clock on the night stand. It was three in the morning, not a time to expect good news. Quickly, he put on his robe and headed down the stairs. Glenda, his wife, wasn't far behind.

When Bobby opened the door, there stood Leah, his only daughter, accompanied by John Andrews, an officer with Hickory Grove's police department and a member of Boiling Springs Church.

"Preacher, I'm sorry to wake you up at this time of night, but I decided to bring Leah home instead of taking her down to the police station. Leah and her boyfriend let their little party get out of hand. I picked them up down at Veteran's Park. They were swimming in the fountain and singing at the top of their lungs. Some of the folks who live near the park heard them and called the station. They really ought to be booked for disturbing the peace and public intoxication, but unless somebody complains, we can save everybody the embarrassment by not letting this go public."

As Leah stood dripping wet in the doorway, sobriety did not stand with her. She refused to look up, seemingly fixated on some imaginary spot on the floor. She reeked with the smell of alcohol, and though Officer Andrews held her arm, she had difficulty standing without swaying.

"John, I really appreciate this. I really do," said Bobby. "I don't think it'd help our church's reputation if the people of Hickory Grove knew that their preacher's kid got drunk and became a public nuisance. You can be sure I'll handle this in a way that'll make this girl understand the consequences of her actions."

With that, the officer said good night to his pastor. Bobby Stone then led his daughter into the house and closed the door.

—⚇—

"Young lady," said Bobby in a voice way too loud for intoxicated ears. "What am I gonna do with you? I've taught you better than this. How dare you bring disgrace to your mother, to me, and to the folks down at the church!"

"Shut up," barked Leah, in a voice that exploded with years of repressed anger. "You don't care about me. You don't even care about Mother. All you care about is the reputation of Boiling Springs Church."

"Listen here, Leah. I'll not have any of that kind of talk in this house . . ."

But before he could finish his sentence, Leah pulled away, swaggered into her bedroom, and slammed the door. Bobby started after her until Glenda stopped him.

"Bobby, leave her alone. You're angry. She's drunk, and both of you are bound to say things you'll regret in the morning."

"But that girl can't talk to us that way. She's gonna . . ."

"She's gonna what?" interrupted Glenda. "I'll tell you what she's gonna do. She's gonna leave home, move in with her boyfriend, Richard, and then what are you gonna do about the reputation of Boiling Springs Church? Like I said, "Just let things cool down and we'll sort them out in the morning."

For a moment, the irate pastor just glared at his wife, and then without another word, he retreated to his study; and that's where he spent the rest of the night.

—m—

Bobby Stone had been pastor of Boiling Springs Church for twenty years. It was the only church he'd pastored since graduating from Midway Bible College.

Bobby was one of those preachers who "preached hard on sin," and his sermons were often stern and severe. When he preached, he was loud. Some said he had the passion of uncompromising integrity. Others said he just sounded angry.

When somebody would refer to the Boiling Springs Church as a conservative church, he'd quickly correct them. "We're not conservative," he'd say. "We're just biblical."

As a child, Leah was her father's pride and joy. Few children were born with a voice more beautiful than hers. As a preschooler, Rev. Stone would bring her up to the front of the church and let her sing. The congregation would applaud, and Stone would beam as she sang their gospel favorites.

As Leah grew older, she continued singing in church. During special seasons of the year, she was always the featured soloist. On the 4th of July, there was not a dry eye in the house when she'd sing "I'm Proud to be An American," and during the Christmas season, the folks at Boiling Springs always expected Leah to bless them with her rendition of "O Holy Night."

But things began to change once Leah entered high school. The tensions between Leah and her father increased daily. She was hungry for adolescent freedom, but her father was intent on keeping strict control of everything she did.

In her senior year, Leah started dating Richard Branson. Richard was the epitome of everything her father preached against. He drank, he smoked, his language was crude, and the only time he'd been in a church was during his grandfather's funeral.

When Bobby Stone found out about his daughter's new boyfriend, he strictly forbade her to see him. Of course, his prohibition only fueled her desire to rebel, and she did everything she could to sneak out and meet him when her father wasn't looking.

Once she graduated, the hostilities between Leah and her father only escalated. Instead of sneaking out to meet Richard, she brazenly ignored her father's wishes, seeing him whenever she wanted. Sometimes she'd be gone days at a time without her parents knowing when she would return; and when she was home, most of her time was spent arguing with her father; and, of course, her absence at Boiling Springs Church was noticed by everybody in Hickory Grove.

Prior to meeting Richard, Leah planned to attend Midway Bible College - she was even promised a music scholarship - but now she had no intention of attending Midway or any other school. The only thing she cared about was spending time with Richard.

—m—

It was late Saturday morning when Leah finally came out of her room. She was relieved when she glanced out at the driveway and noticed her father's car was gone. He was probably at church – as usual. When she looked into the den, she saw her mother curled up on the couch reading a book.

"Can I get you something to eat?" asked Glenda as she marked the page and closed her book.

"No thanks, Mom. My stomach's still a little queasy."

"Why don't you come over here and sit down. I think we need to talk."

"I don't want to talk," she said, bristling at the thought of another confrontation.

"Listen, I'm not going to judge you nor am I going to argue about Richard. I just want to find out what's going on in the heart and mind of my daughter."

As Leah looked at her mother's face, she saw a mixture of compassion and worry in her eyes. She knew her mother didn't approve of her new lifestyle, but at the same time, she knew her mother really cared.

"Okay Mom," she said as she scooted up next to her on the couch. "I've wanted to talk to you for some time, but it seems like whenever I try to talk, Dad just gets mad and all we do is yell."

"Leah, I'm hurt and I'm worried, but I don't want to yell. I just want us to talk. I just want to know what's going on in your life."

"Mom, I know you and Dad don't like Richard, but I'm in love with him and he's in love with me. Have you all forgotten what it's like to be in love?"

Slowly a smile crept across Glenda's face. "Honey, we still know what it's like to be in love. Believe it or not, your dad was a real romancer in his day. And while he may not seem that way now, I know he loves me deeply; and he loves you, too."

"I'm not so sure of that," said Leah. "I'm not sure he really loves me at all. I've always felt like I had to earn his love, always felt like I had to live up to his exacting Christian standards. And now, since I'm not doing things his way, I feel like he doesn't really care for me at all."

"That's not so, Leah. I know your dad is stern and strict, but underneath that hard surface is a heart that loves you a lot."

For the next few moments, neither woman spoke. Both seemed to be looking for words that would convey love instead of anger, words that would bring them together instead of pushing them apart.

"Mom," began Leah in a softer, gentler tone. "I need to tell you something."

"What is it?" Glenda asked, almost knowing what words would be coming next.

"Richard and I have decided to live together."

"Live together - without getting married?"

"Yes, Mom. He's rented a small house on the south side of town, and we plan to make it our home."

"Are you planning to be married eventually?" asked Glenda.

"Someday, maybe," said Leah; "but for the time being, we just want to be near each other."

For the longest time, Glenda just sat there, not being sure of what to say. Finally, she reached out and caressed Leah's hand, knowing that the next words she spoke must be chosen carefully.

"Leah, you know neither your father nor I can condone what you're doing. We believe in marriage because we believe real love is a love of commitment. Still, I realize we cannot stop you, and while I wish you would make a different choice, I will continue to love you no matter what you choose. You are my daughter, and nothing you do can cause me to stop loving you."

For the longest time, Glenda simply held her daughter's hand. Words seemed unnecessary to convey the love that Leah and her mother shared.

Later that day, Leah broke the news to her father, and his reaction was anything but compassionate.

"I can't believe this," he said. "I can't believe you've turned your back on all the things we've taught you. I knew Richard was bad news from the day you started seeing him. And now, look what he's done. Your sin and rebellion will be the talk of the town. You will be disgraced; not only you, but our entire family will be disgraced. How do you expect me to lead the ministry of Boiling Springs Church if my daughter turns her back on the truths we hold so dear?"

"You don't even care about me, do you?" protested Leah. "All you care about is your reputation and the reputation of Boiling Springs Church. In all those 'truths you hold so dear,' is there no room for the truth of grace and love? For years, I've known about your truth. I've known that you love that church more than you've ever loved me, and to be quite honest, I can't wait until I live with someone who loves me for who I am, not for who he wants me to be! As far as I'm concerned, I don't care if I ever see you or your church again!"

Even as the words fell from her lips, Leah regretted having said them, and for the first time ever, she saw her father speechless, wounded and broken under the weight of his disappointment and pain.

Over the next few days, Leah and her father were strangers living under the same roof. The arguing was over and the only conversations they shared were conversations of practical necessity.

A week later, Leah left home and moved in with Richard. Her mother would visit and call on a regular basis but, by his silence and by his absence, her father made it perfectly clear he wanted nothing to do with his daughter as long as she chose to live a life of sin.

Needless to say, the stress between Bobby and his daughter spilled over into his relationship with his wife. At times, Glenda begged Bobby to put his pride behind him and become a part of his daughter's life, but Bobby's reply was always the same. "I didn't choose that life for her and I'm not going to condone it. If she wants to get her life right and return to God, she knows where I am. But as long as she chooses to live a life of sin, she'll do it without my blessing."

One of the most popular services at the Boiling Springs Church was its annual Candlelight Christmas Eve service. On Christmas Eve, the Boiling Springs choir always presented a Christmas musical that included favorite hymns and carols. At the end of the service, the entire congregation would join in the singing while they passed candle light from one to another.

On this particular Christmas Eve, the sanctuary was packed. In fact, a few of the latecomers had to stand at the back of the church. As always, the choir ushered in the celebration of Christ's birth with the most beautiful music of the season.

After they sang, the lights were dimmed and a couple of the deacons began the ceremony of passing the candle light. As the worshippers passed the candle light from one to the other, Pastor Stone began reading from John 1:

In the beginning was the Word, and the Word was with God, and the Word was God. The same was in the beginning with God.

All things were made by him; and without him was not anything made that was made.

In him was life; and the life was the light of men. And the light shineth in darkness; and the darkness comprehended it not. . . . That was the true Light, which lighteth every man that cometh into the world.

He was in the world, and the world was made by him, and the world knew him not. He came unto his own . . . (Stone pauses and clears his throat*). He . . . he . . . he came unto his own . . . and . . . and his own received him not.*

Before he realized what was happening, the truth of the passage captured Bobby's heart. On that first Christmas, Jesus was God's gift, a gift of love given in the form of a baby, but God's baby was rejected, rejected not by strangers but rejected by the baby's own family.

Now, 2,000 years later, this passage was being lived out again. Eighteen years ago, God had sent another beautiful gift of love, a gift of love in the form of his own dear daughter, but in his arrogance and pride, he had rejected God's gift of love. As The Scriptures said, "*She came to her own and her own received her not.*"

As Bobby Stone stood there, he was thankful the sanctuary was darkened; else the congregation would have seen the tears streaming down his face. Sensing that his pastor was not going to be able to finish the passage, Jack Leland, the pastor's assistant, picked up where the pastor left off.

He came unto his own and his own received him not, but as many as received him, to them gave he power to become the sons of God, even to them that believe on his name.

When he finished reading the passage, a silence crept across the congregation, but only for a moment. Soon the silence was broken by a familiar voice that came from the back of the church.

Oh, Holy Night, the stars are brightly shining, it is the night of the dear Savior's birth.

As Leah's pure voice echoed off the rafters of the church, she and her mother slowly walked down the center aisle. When Bobby saw them coming, he almost ran down from the pulpit area to join them, and when he got to where they were, Leah fell into her father's open arms.

Then, in a move that surprised even his wife, Bobby joined in the singing.

Fall on your knees. Oh hear, the angel voices. Oh, night divine. Oh night, when Christ was born. Oh night, divine. Oh night, oh night divine.

Bobby Stone was never the same after that night. Instead of being known for his stern, hard sermons, he became known as a preacher of love, an ambassador of grace. And while his preaching wasn't as loud as it had been, a lot of folks said he preached with more power, and rightly so. *For as many as received him, to them gave he power to become the sons of God, even to them that believe on his name.*

six

O Little Town of Jefferson

But you, Bethlehem Ephrathah, though you are small among the clans of Judah, out of you will come for me one who will be ruler over Israel, whose origins are from of old, from ancient times.
(Micah 5:2 NIV)

Christmas Eve. The church office closed at noon. I was alone, trying desperately to finish preparing Sunday's sermon so I could spend a few minutes with my family. Then I heard the knocking. Someone was at the outer office door.

My office door was closed, so I slowly cracked it open and peaked out the outer office door to see who was knocking. When I glanced through the glass, I saw the face of a man, and I knew, in an instant, why he came knocking. He was a transient, one of the poor people who had come to the office to ask for help.

To be perfectly honest, I didn't want to deal with him. I had already dealt with several benevolent cases that day. That's why my sermon was unfinished. Dealing with benevolent cases takes so much time, and dealing with this one would only make me get home that much later.

A lot of people come by the week before Christmas. Some are legitimate, but some come on Christmas Eve to play the Christmas Eve guilt game. They know Christmas Eve is a good time to play on your sympathies. Who's going to say "no" to a beggar on Christmas Eve? I mean, that's like spittin' in the face of baby Jesus.

Finally I decided I wasn't going to be duped by this Christmas Eve con man, so I slowly shut my office door hoping he would go away, but he didn't. Instead, he kept knocking, and with each knock I felt a new level of guilt.

Finally, when I realized he wasn't going away, I let him in the office.

As I looked at the man, I felt sorry for him. He wasn't like the usual Christmas Eve con man. He was polite and humble, and it was obvious he was embarrassed to ask for help.

My voice softened a little as I asked, "What can I do for you?"

He told me his name was Joe and that he and his wife, Maria, were headed to New York to spend Hanukah with relatives. When they got to Exit 417, their car broke down and they had to have it towed to a mechanic here in Jefferson.

"Sir, I've spent all the money I had on the towing bill. I'm not even sure where I'll find the money to fix the car. That's why I've come to you. My wife and I need a place to spend the night, but we have no money. The people at the Sunoco station said your church might help us."

He sounded legitimate, but I was still a little suspicious. Typically, I would have called around to verify the guy's story, but since I was already behind on my sermon, I decided to forget the formalities and try to get him some help.

First, I called Samaritan House, our local homeless shelter, and asked if I could send the couple there for the night. The host was polite but told me every bed was filled.

Next, I started calling hotels at Exit 417. I called the Holiday Inn Express, the Comfort Inn, Ramada Inn and every other hotel I could think of, but in each case I got the same reply. "I'm sorry. It's Christmas Eve and we're full."

When I hung up from calling the last hotel, I was really frustrated. I was making no progress with this transient, nor was I any closer to finishing my sermon.

Perhaps Joe sensed my frustration because he stood and walked toward the door. "Sir, I'm sorry," he said. "I didn't mean to put you to so much trouble. You need not worry about my wife and me. We'll find a place."

Instantly, I felt ashamed. Here was a man who had a legitimate need, and I was making him feel bad for being destitute.

"I'm sorry," I said. "I'm not upset with you. I'm just frustrated for not having time to finish my sermon."

Shyly, he smiled and said, "I bet you're a good preacher. Though we are Jewish, if we're around here on Sunday, my wife and I would love to come and hear you preach."

As I looked at the man's face, I realized he wasn't just trying to butter me up. He was sincere, and his sincerity made me feel guiltier than ever for my uncaring attitude.

As he stood there, I kept trying to think of a place for him to spend the night. Then I remembered the missionary house, the old house used by our church to provide temporary lodging for furloughed missionaries. No one had used it for several months, and it probably needed a thorough cleaning, but even with the gathered dust, it had to be better than having no place at all.

"I think I know where you and your wife could spend the night," I said. Our church owns a little house we use as a temporary residence for missionaries, but it's vacant right now. I'm not sure what kind of shape it's in, but I can let you spend the night there if you're willing."

Instantly, his face brightened. "Oh, yes sir. We'd be honored to stay in your missionary house, regardless of its condition."

Quickly, Joe and I left the office headed for the missionary house, but before we got to the front door of the church, Joe said, "Pastor, let me get my wife. She's in your sanctuary. She went there to pray."

A moment later, Joe walked out of the sanctuary accompanied by Maria, his wife; and when I looked at her, I could hardly believe what I saw. Joe's wife was pregnant - very pregnant. She looked as if she could have her baby any day.

When I saw the condition of Maria, I urged him to come home with me. "We've got a house full of out-of-town family, but I'm sure we can find a place for you and your wife.

Firmly, Joe refused my offer. "The missionary house is a gracious offer," he said. "We'll be fine there. Your house is full. The missionary house is empty. I think the missionary house will be perfect!"

When we got to the missionary house, I apologized for its condition. It was really dusty and the linens on the bed were old and tattered. When I turned on the thermostat, the old system coughed and kicked and then gave up the ghost. Fortunately, I found a small electric space heater that would keep the bedroom tolerably warm.

As I apologized, Joe interrupted me and said, "Don't apologize. This is perfect. We'll do quite well here. The bed will be just fine and this old bed spread will keep us warm."

After I got them situated, I went back to my office feeling a little guilty for leaving them in such a humble place – but hey, at least they had a place.

Thankfully, I didn't have any more interruptions the rest of the afternoon, and after finishing my Christmas sermon, I headed home.

It must have been about ten thirty Friday evening when I got the call. It was John Martin, our church custodian.

"Pastor, I'm sorry to bother you this late at night, but I wasn't sure who else to call."

"What's wrong?" I asked.

"Well, as I was coming back from our Sunday School Class Christmas party, I noticed lights on in the missionary house, so I stopped to see what was going on. When I unlocked the door, I found two transients in the upstairs bedroom."

Quickly I interrupted, "I'm sorry, John. I guess I should have told you. I put them there this afternoon. They needed a place to spend the night and since all the local places were filled, I decided to let them stay in the missionary house."

"Well, that's not the problem," said John with an uneasy sense of urgency.

"What is the problem?" I asked.

"It's the woman. When I went in there to check on them, she was in labor. Now, pastor, I know a lot about fixin' houses and takin' care of churches, but I don't know nothin' bout birthin' no babies. That's why I called you."

I wanted to tell him I didn't know nothin' bout birthin' no babies either, but instead I told him to stay with them until I could get there.

Before I left the house, I called my neighbor, Dr. Jeff Kim, and asked him to go with me. By the time Jeff and I got to the missionary house, everything was over. Just minutes before we arrived, the baby was born, a healthy baby boy. Dr. Kim checked out Maria and the baby and reported everyone was fine.

As he pulled out his cell phone, he said, "Looks like everybody's fine, but let's get you over to the hospital just to make sure."

"No, don't call the hospital," the mother said. "We'll be just fine here."

"But, ma'am," protested Dr. Kim, "you really need to let us put you and your baby in a warm, sanitary place, at least overnight."

Firmly Joe replied, "Doctor, I know you mean well, but we're private people and will not be entering the hospital. You good people have already done enough. We'll be quite satisfied to keep mother and baby here."

"We can't make you go to the hospital," replied Dr. Kim, "but you make sure to keep that baby and mother warm. You hear?"

When I saw they wouldn't go to the hospital, I again urged them to come home with me. "My home is not far away. You'd be much more comfortable there. Besides, you don't need to stay here where it's dusty and drafty."

Again, the man politely but firmly refused. "We really don't want to be a bother. Please, go on home to your family and don't worry about us. We'll be fine here."

So Dr. Kim and I left the missionary house reluctantly. Neither of us wanted to leave them there, but the couple made it perfectly clear they would go nowhere else.

As I walked out of the house and headed to my car, I looked up into the sky and glanced at the moon. Dr. Kim noticed it, too. For some reason, it seemed to shine brighter than usual, and the bright light seemed to focus on the place where the baby was born.

―⚬⚬⚬―

As you might imagine, it didn't take long for news about the missionary house baby to spread like wildfire. Everybody in town was thrilled about the baby's birth.

Early Saturday morning, when I went to the missionary house to check on the transients, there were all sorts of folks welcoming the new arrival. As I walked into the house, I noticed that the entire house was warm and comfortable. John Martin had gotten the heating contractor out of bed and he had come early to fix the furnace. A reporter from the *Standard Banner* was there, and some ladies from our church. The church ladies were presenting the new baby with crocheted blankets and handmade outfits. You would have thought a king had been born here in Jefferson. People from all over town came bringing gifts. By the end of the day, the little bedroom was filled with diapers, baby formula, and a whole assortment of baby clothes.

Later that day, I went to pick up the couple's old car from the mechanic. He, too, had heard about the remarkable birth and wouldn't accept any payment for his work. For some reason, everybody in Jefferson seemed to think this newborn baby was something special.

―⚬⚬⚬―

Last night, just after sunset, I went to check on the family again. While I was there, a group of children from the Catholic Church came by to sing Christmas carols. The children were so cute, maybe a dozen of them, all dressed up like angels. With pride they sang "Away in the Manger," "Joy to the World," and "Oh, Little Town of Bethlehem." As they sang, the same moon that had shone so brightly the night before rose again and beamed through the window to the place where the baby lay.

Early Sunday morning, I went by the missionary house to check on the new parents and baby one more time before going to church. When I drove up to the house, I noticed the old car was not there. When I went inside, I discovered the family had left during the night. Surprisingly, the missionary house was spotless and in much better shape than it was when I had taken them there Friday. Joe had even repaired some areas we had neglected for years. Obviously, he was an expert carpenter.

As I looked down at the mattress, I saw a note, written on the back of a *Pampers* box top. The note said,

Dear Dr. Wilder. I'm sorry we will not be at church to hear your sermon Sunday, but we felt it was time to go see our family. Thanks for everything, and please thank all the good folks in this little town of Jefferson.

And then at the bottom of the note he left this strange message:

For you, oh Jefferson, though you are small among the cities and towns, out of you will come one who will be ruler over all the world, whose origins are from of old, from ancient times.

Did this really happen? Of course it did. But it didn't happen to me, and it didn't happen in Jefferson, Tennessee. It happened to shepherds, innkeepers and townsfolk in another little town, the Little Town of Bethlehem.

But it could have happened in Jefferson. Yes, the birth of the Messiah could have happened in our little town. For sometimes God does his most significant work in the little towns, in those out-of-the-way places, places like Bethlehem and like Jefferson, Tennessee.

So keep your eyes open and your heart full of love because someday, God might do something in the place where you live. Yes, God might do something with innkeepers, farmers, and wise men and women like you and like me.

So the next time you sing the carol, don't be afraid to change a word or two because nobody knows where God may perform his next Christmas miracle. It might be in the little town of Bethlehem or it could be in the little town of Jefferson. So don't be afraid to change a few words when you sing,

O little town of Jefferson, how still we see thee lie,
Above thy deep and dreamless sleep, the silent stars go by.
Yet in thy dark streets shineth, the everlasting light.
The hopes and fears of all the years are met in thee, tonight.

seven

In Search of the Missing Christ Child

> *When Jesus spoke again to the people, he said, "I am the light of the world. Whoever follows me will never walk in darkness, but will have the light of life."*
> *(John 8:12 NIV)*

No six-year-old could have been more excited than Susie McFadden. It was Christmas Eve and she could hardly wait for the fun to begin.

The McFaddens had special family traditions they faithfully observed every Christmas Eve. The evening always began with a special meal. Mrs. McFadden would begin early in the day to prepare the annual Christmas Eve feast. Christmas just didn't seem like Christmas until the house was filled with the aroma of honey-cured ham, cinnamon cider, and freshly baked muffins.

After the meal, the family always went to the living room to set up their special nativity. The McFadden's nativity was unlike any other. It was over two hundred years old, an ancient heirloom that traced back through several generations of Irish ancestors.

Every piece of the nativity was made from hand-painted porcelain. The figures looked so life-like you almost expected them to walk and talk when set in their appropriate places. Despite their age, the pieces were still in excellent condition.

Besides opening presents, Susie's favorite part of Christmas was setting up the nativity. Of all the characters, she liked the baby Jesus best.

As usual, the family gathered around the table, and after Mr. McFadden said the blessing, everyone eagerly began to devour the meal. Susie ate faster than the others because she was so excited about setting up the nativity.

Excusing herself from the table, Susie went into the living room and opened the big, old, wooden chest where the nativity was kept. As she opened the lid, the first character she saw was the baby Jesus. Carefully, she picked it up and hugged it as though it were alive. Then she carried it over to the fireplace to put it on the mantel.

But just as she got to the fireplace, Susie tripped on an old piece of carpet, dropping the figurine on the stone-covered hearth. When the porcelain figure hit the hearth, it shattered into dozens of pieces. That's when Susie broke into uncontrollable tears.

Quickly, the rest of the family ran into the room to see what had happened.

"I broke the baby Jesus," cried Susie. "And how can we have Christmas if we don't have a baby Jesus?"

For the longest time, the family stood by the hearth in shock. All of them were devastated at the loss of this family heirloom. And Susie was right, there was no use putting up the nativity scene if you didn't have the baby Jesus.

Don McFadden, Susie's father, tried to console his heartbroken daughter. "Honey," he said, "let's go ahead and set up the rest of the characters and maybe we can find another baby Jesus."

"Where will we find another one?" cried Susie.

"I don't know," replied Don, "but I just believe something will work out."

So the McFadden family got busy setting up the rest of the nativity scene. They set up the stable with the cows, the oxen and several sheep. Then carefully they arranged the wisemen and shepherds, putting them on the outer edges, leaving room for the manger and the baby Jesus. Then they placed Mary and Joseph in the middle, beside the empty manger.

Everything looked just right except for the empty manger. As Susie took one glance at the finished product, she again burst into tears and ran up to her room crying, "It's no good. It's just no good without the baby Jesus." And while none of the other family members admitted it, they all knew she was right.

For the next hour or so, the family did everything they could to find a suitable replacement for the broken baby Jesus. They tried a figurine from a neighbor's nativity set but the baby Jesus was too small and looked out of place. They tried some of Susie's dolls, but all of them were too big and none of them really looked like baby Jesus. Finally, they decided that when they got home from the Christmas Eve service, they would take the set down and hunt for a replacement before next Christmas.

No one said a word as the McFaddens drove to church for the Christmas Eve service. In fact, the only sound that could be heard was the occasional sniffle of a teary-eyed, broken-hearted little girl. Susie didn't stop crying until her mother handed her one of the candles she would later light in the service. Susie always liked holding the lighted candle, and she soon remembered how pretty the church looked when everyone's candle was lit.

The Christmas Eve service was just like Susie remembered, and when time came for everyone to light their candle, she soon forgot how upset she was over the broken baby Jesus.

As the church glowed from the light of the candles, the preacher read these words from the Bible: *In Him was life, and the life was the light of all men. And the light shines in the darkness, and the darkness could not extinguish it.*

After reading the verses, the preacher explained that before Jesus was born, the world was trapped in the darkness of sin. No one could really be happy because sin was like a dark sadness that hung over their lives. But when Jesus came, He came as a light to chase all the darkness and sadness away so that no one would have to be trapped by the darkness of sin.

As Susie held her candle, she looked at its glowing flame and thought to herself, "Maybe Jesus doesn't want me to feel dark and sad because I broke the baby Jesus. Maybe Jesus wants to be my light and chase away the darkness and sadness from me."

As Susie left church that night, she wasn't sure why, but she knew she felt better. Something in the candlelight made her know that everything would be all right.

When the McFaddens got home, Susie went straight into the living room to take one more look at the incomplete nativity. Moments later the rest of the family heard her gleeful cries, "I found Him, I found Him, I found Him," she yelled. "Everybody come see the baby Jesus. I found him and I've put him in the manger."

One by one each family member rushed into the darkened living room to see what Susie had found. On top of the mantle, the nativity scene was arranged just as it had been earlier; but one thing was noticeably different. In the middle of the scene, wedged between Joseph and Mary was a small candle, a left over from the Christmas Eve service. When Susie's father lit the candle, the light from that single candle enveloped the whole nativity scene in a divine-like radiance. Everything looked so peaceful. All the characters seemed to smile with joy. Never had the old nativity looked so beautiful.

As the candlelight reflected from Susie eyes, she declared, "It's just like the preacher read in the Bible. Baby Jesus didn't come to earth just to be a baby doll in a manger; He came to earth to be our light. I'm sorry I broke the other baby Jesus, but to tell the truth, I think this one's much prettier than the other one ever was."

Evidently, the rest of the McFadden family agreed with Susie, for after that year, they never tried to find another replacement for the broken baby Jesus. Instead, they decided that the best baby Jesus wasn't a baby after all; the best baby Jesus was the light, yes, the true light which, coming into the world, enlightens everyone's heart.

eight

The Real Reason for the Season

> . . . *The Lord does not look at the things people look at. People look at the outward appearance, but the Lord looks at the heart.*
> (1 Samuel 16:7 NIV)

The room was buzzing with excitement as 400 plus people crowded into the fellowship hall of New Haven Community Church. New Haven Church was located about a mile off the intersection of Interstates 95 and 91, a two hour drive from the heart of New York City. And though it was the middle of May, everyone had one thing on their minds – Christmas.

Pastor Bradley Jacobs walked to the speaker's stand and called everyone to order.

"I'm glad to see all of you here," he began, "especially those of you who don't attend our church. Obviously, the problem we're combating is much bigger than any one church can solve, so I'm glad to see we'll be working on this together.

"Now let me address why we're here. We're here to put together a Christmas celebration that will outshine and outperform anything conceived of by the merchants of our area. When Christmas comes this year, we want people to look at the manger instead of gawking at the brightly-lit store displays. We want to draw people away from spending millions of dollars on things they don't need or can't afford. Instead, we want to draw them to what they need most, a relationship with the

Savior who was born on Christmas Day. Yes, this year, we want people to realize their treasure lies not on the shelves of Macy's or along the aisle of Best Buy. We want them to realize their true treasure lies in the bounty of heaven. Yes, this year, we're reclaiming Christmas for Christ, snatching it from the greedy, little hands of those who would use our Savior to fill their pockets with cash."

Almost in unison, "Amens" resounded from all over the room. Of course, most of Jacobs' members had heard his stump speech on several occasions, but they didn't mind hearing it again. His passion was contagious, and when they heard him get excited about his war against the commercialization of Christmas, it made them want to join his army and defeat the "greedy, godless mob."

Quickly, Jacobs got down to business.

"In order to be successful, we need to divide our work into four different Success Teams. First, we need the Pageant Team. Your job will be to write, produce, and perform the most impressive Christmas pageant ever presented on the face of the earth. When people realize just how wonderful and massive this pageant will be, they will quickly turn their backs on the pricey showroom displays and come to bow their knees at the manger of our Savior.

Now, those of you talented with gifts of drama, music, staging, and lighting need to be a part of the Pageant Team that will meet with Chairwoman Isabel Monchichi in Room 121.

"Next we need the Publicity Team. Yes, we need to publicize this event in every way conceivable. Well-crafted commercials need to air regularly on every TV station between Thanksgiving Day and Christmas Eve. We need to run ads in the newspapers and on Interstate billboards as well. I don't have to remind you that thousands of travelers go up and down Interstates 95 and 91 every day. And as they travel, they need to be enticed to attend the 'greatest show on earth.'

"Now, those of you who want to be part of the Publicity Team need to meet with Chairman Paul Pressman in Room 125."

"Then we need an Arrangements Team. We are honored to host the show in our massive new church auditorium. It seats almost nine thousand; so if we have three shows on December 23rd and three more on December 24th, we can bring this blessed event to over 50,000 people. Obviously, we will need people to help with parking, ushers to help with seating, and a host of others to handle everything from first aid to security. Those who wish to serve on the Arrangements Team need meet with Chairman Jamison Hodges in Room 131.

"And then, last but not least, we need a Financial Resources Team. Conducting something of this magnitude will be extremely expensive, and that shouldn't surprise us. If the profit-making crowd is willing to spend millions to get people into their stores, should we not be willing to do the same to get people into the church? We need to raise money for developing the sets and costumes for the pageant, and we need money to pay the members of the hundred piece orchestra that will support this event. We need even more money to purchase advertising on TV, newspapers and billboards. Something of this magnitude will require us to raise over 3 million dollars, so we need an army of courageous businessmen and businesswomen who will help us raise the cash.

"So those of you who will serve on the Financial Resources Team need to go to Room 134 to meet with Chairman Rodney Strong."

Over the next couple of hours, each Success Team met to plan the event that would defeat the godless profit-makers and refocus the eyes of all New Haven on the real reason for the Christmas season.

—m—

After the initial flurry of excitement, the job of putting together this massive event turned into long hours of hard work. It took Isabel Monchichi over two months to write the stage play; but when it was read by the members of her Success Team, the entire group decided it was nothing short of a Broadway spectacular.

The problem came, not in writing the stage play, but in casting it. For weeks, Monchichi's committee auditioned hundreds who wanted to perform on stage. The small roles were easy to fill. Shepherds, wisemen, and townsfolk were cast in a matter of days, and the 200-voice choir of angels came together without much difficulty. But casting the major roles with solos, the roles of Mary,

Joseph, Elizabeth, and Gabriel, became the director's nightmare. Most of those who auditioned had satisfactory voices, but few had the talent required to sing on the big stage. Still, almost everyone who auditioned felt like they were "God-called" for their part.

When the final decisions were made, several singers claimed that the members of New Haven Community Church had gotten preferential treatment. A few even went to their pastors and suggested their churches should withdraw from the project. Thankfully, only one church, Little Bethlehem Church, withdrew because of the casting controversy.

Still, the most contentious issue regarding the casting had nothing to do with the soloists. The biggest fight came over who would play the part of the baby Jesus. Among the hundreds involved in the production, six of the women were pregnant with boy babies who had due dates between Thanksgiving and Christmas, and each of those mothers demanded that her child be cast as the Baby Jesus.

Finally, in an attempt to give each child a fair chance, Isabel decided that the third baby born after Thanksgiving would get the role. She seemed to think her method of threes best reflected the work of the Holy Trinity. Unfortunately, the pregnant mothers were not as impressed with her theological design.

The Financial Resources Success Team got off to a good start, raising almost $500,000 from persons participating in the pageant; but when they started asking local business owners to make contributions, they ran into a stone wall. Most of the business owners made their largest profits during the Christmas season. Obviously, they weren't excited about supporting a program aimed at luring away their customers.

In the end, Rodney Strong and his committee discovered the most generous donors by making the short trip down to New York City. Strong and his committee members met with the Downtown Retailers Association and assured them that, because of the grand pageant, shopping would become unpopular in New Haven and, therefore, New Haven customers would likely make their purchases by coming to New York City. The rationale seemed to work with New York retailers, and by early October, Strong and his committee had raised over 2 million dollars.

By Thanksgiving weekend, the project was gaining steam. Pageant rehearsals were going well and the staging at New Haven Church looked like one of the most elaborate sets on Broadway.

Contributions had picked up considerably and the Financial Resources Team had almost reached its goal. All over town people began seeing the billboards and advertisements. Everywhere you turned in New Haven, you found people talking about the upcoming show.

All in all, it seemed like the Christmas show was going to be a success. Granted, there were still a lot of last minute details to be ironed out, but nothing seemed beyond the control of Pastor Bradley Jacobs and the leaders of his hard working success teams.

On December eighteenth, as Pastor Jacobs watched one of his TV ads, he didn't like what he saw in the long-range weather forecast that followed.

"Over the next few days, a low pressure system will head to us from the South, passing just off the New England Coast. Depending on the timing of the storm, we could see some severe weather in our area. Of course, at this stage, it's too early to predict. If the front gains speed, it could drop just an inch or two of snow before it moves out, giving us a beautiful White Christmas. Stay tuned here at Weather Central as we watch this system and give you more details as the week progresses."

Of all his plans and prayers, a Nor'easter had been the last thing on Bradley Jacobs' mind. Over the months, he had been able to control the musical production, the advertising and even the fund raising, but the weather was one thing he could not control. Or could he?

Jacobs was a man of prayer, and he concluded that since this pageant was intended to bring glory to God, surely the prayers of God's people would persuade God to take care of the weather.

Immediately, Jacobs started calling all the pastors who were participating in the project, asking them to call upon their people to pray. On the next day, which was Sunday, Jacobs announced there would be a twenty-four hour prayer vigil at the church, and if God's people would come and pray, God would surely take care of the storm. Following their pastor's request, hundreds of people came to church over the next twenty-four hours asking God to hold back the weather so that they could conduct the pageant.

On December twenty-second, the weather forecast was not encouraging at all. "It looks like that weather front coming down from the Maine Coast will collide with the low coming up from the South. I hate to be the bearer of bad tidings, especially during the holiday season, but I think we're in for some of the nastiest weather we've seen in years. The rain will begin tonight, but by tomorrow morning the rain will turn into a freezing sleet that could dump as much as a quarter inch of ice in our area. The ice will eventually turn to snow, and with forty to fifty mile an hour winds, we're likely to see blizzard conditions. We could get as much as fifteen to twenty inches of snow on top of the ice before Christmas Eve. The National Weather Service has issued a Winter Storm Warning and is asking people to stay in their homes except for emergency travel. Along with closed highways and chilling temperatures, you can expect massive power outages. Stayed tuned here at Weather Central for any breaking news on this storm that is already being called "The Blizzard of the Century."

As Pastor Jacobs heard the words, he found himself speechless. "This just couldn't be happening," he thought. "Why would God let them down when they had put so much effort into helping people see the real reason for the season? Why had God ignored their prayers? Why had the Lord disrupted their plans? And worst of all, what was he going to say to all those who had spent so much time and money putting together an extravaganza that was never going to happen?"

Over the next twenty-four hours, everything in New Haven screeched to a halt, a city paralyzed by The Blizzard of the Century. Driving was impossible, except for those who had four-wheel-drive vehicles equipped with snow chains. No home or business had electric service except those with emergency generators. In one house after another, people huddled together, covered with blankets, trying to stay warm until power was restored.

Interstates 95 and 91 were virtual parking lots filled with holiday travelers who had no idea how long they would be stranded in their cars. The situation was quickly turning from being uncomfortable to being dangerous. Unless these stranded travelers were rescued and brought to safety, many of them could literally freeze to death.

Surprisingly, the only utility in the area not entirely affected by the storm was cell phone service, but even that was undependable. With so many travelers calling for help, the few lines that were open often were busy. Still, if you tried long enough, you could usually get your call through.

As Bradley Jacobs and his wife sat near the fireplace in their den, his cell phone rang. When he answered it, he found himself talking to Jimmy Johnson, Director of the area's Emergency Management Team.

"Rev. Jacobs," Johnson began. "We've got a serious situation here. We've got hundreds of stranded folks out on Interstates 91 and 95. If we can't get them to safety, I don't know what's gonna' happen to them.

"I'm told you have an emergency generator that can provide power to the day school in your church. If we can find a way to get some of these folks to your church, would you allow them to stay there for the next couple days?"

Without thinking twice, Jacobs agreed to let his church be a refuge for the strangers. "I'll send a vehicle to pick you up," said Johnson "and it'll take you to your church so you can help prepare."

Minutes later, Jacobs heard the snow chains on the four-wheel-drive vehicle coming toward his home. When he got into the car, Johnson welcomed him.

"Pastor, I have no idea how many folks we're talking about and have no idea how we'll care for them once we get them to your church, but I appreciate your willingness to help."

Once Jacobs got to the church, he began calling all the members he could think of who had four wheel drive vehicles and asked those with chains to try to make it to the church, bringing with them any food or supplies they could carry. He also called the pastors he had gotten to know while working on the Christmas pageant and asked them to contact any members who might be able to help.

Before he knew it, church members and folks from the community started streaming into the church's day school. Some had come in chain-equipped vehicles, but most had walked, trudging through the snow, the wind, and the cold.

Within an hour's time, emergency vehicles started dropping off chilled, frightened strangers at the church. When these dazed passengers arrived, they were greeted by smiling people who offered them something hot to drink and a variety of snacks to eat. Before the night was over, 333 people were huddled together in the few warm rooms of the church's day school.

As the crowd of refugees began settling in for the night, Jimmy Johnson walked over and put his hand on the pastor's shoulder. "Pastor," he began, "sorry 'bout your cancelled pageant. I know you folks put an awful lot of work and money into making that pageant the greatest show on earth. But you know what? Your production show couldn't have been any greater than the show I saw here tonight. 'Cause when I look around this room, and see the way your church has cared for these people, I see the real reason for the season more clearly than ever."

So the "Greatest Show Ever" never took place. And despite God's untimely disruption, the people of New Haven did discover the real reason for the season. They saw it not in a multimillion dollar production, but in the sacrificial love of people who really cared. Because in the end, nothing better describes the real reason for the season than selflessly sharing the wonderful gift of God's love.

nine

The Bell Ringer's Friend

For God so loved the world that he gave his only begotten son that whosoever believeth on him shall not perish but have everlasting life.
(John 3:16 KJV)

As Ginny left the mall, she glanced at her watch. "Let's see, it's almost four. If I hurry, I can still beat Fred home from work."

As she pulled into her driveway, she was surprised to see Fred's car already in the garage. Seldom did he get home before six.

"Hi, honey," Ginny called out. No response.

"Hey, honey, I'm home," she repeated, louder this time. Still no response.

As she walked into the den, she finally found Fred. The TV remote was in one hand, a beer in the other. One glance at Fred's face told her something wasn't right. There was a coldness there. His eyes were red and his cheeks were flushed. Obviously, the drink in his hand wasn't his first.

"What's going on here?" she asked.

Without speaking, Fred tossed her the envelope. The letter inside was brief.

Dear Mr. Snyder,

Because of this year's declining sales, we must make a reduction in staff. As of December 7, all middle management positions, including yours, are being eliminated. We regret this necessary action and wish you the best as you secure a position with another employer.

At first, Ginny felt numb as the finality of the words sank in. Then she was angry. "This isn't fair," she cried. "This just isn't fair. You've given that company the best years of your life, and this is the way they pay you back?"

Again, Fred said nothing but continued to change channels on the TV as he finished his drink.

"Aren't you going to say something?" Ginny finally pled.

"What's left to say?" Fred barked. "I'm finished. I mean really finished. Who do you think's gonna hire a sixty-year-old plant manager? I'll be lucky if I can get a job at McDonald's."

Almost from reflex, Ginny reached out to touch her hurting husband, but as she reached toward him, he pulled away. "Fred, don't be that way," she begged. "I know things look bad right now, but we'll find a way."

"You think we're gonna find a way before Christmas?" he growled. "You might as well call up the grandkids and tell 'em not to make the trip this year. Just tell 'em we're fresh out of luck, fresh out of money and fresh out of Christmas."

With that, Fred got up from the recliner, went to the kitchen and got another beer. Then, without a word, he picked up his jacket and walked out the front door, slamming it on his way out.

The air was cold and crisp as Fred walked away from the house. The alcohol had numbed his senses just enough to chase away the chill, but not enough to chase away the pain.

After walking for about an hour, he found himself at the mall. Every inch of the mall's expanse was draped in the trappings of Christmas. Lights blinked as choirs sang. Children ran to whisper secrets to Santa while parents captured the moment with their cameras. In years past, Fred seldom went to the mall, but ever since the grandkids arrived, he found nothing more enjoyable than going to the mall to buy those special gifts for Christmas.

As Fred looked at the decorations, he felt sick inside. This year, buying for grandkids would be somebody else's greatest joy. This year, not buying for grandkids would be Fred Snyder's greatest pain.

As Fred walked by the mall entrance, he heard that familiar sound. "Clang, clang, clink, clang." There stood the familiar volunteer, bell in hand, dutifully standing beside his red tripod, collecting donations for the Salvation Army.

"Clang, clang, clink, clang." Most of the shoppers tried to ignore him as he rang his bell, but occasionally someone would stop and place a quarter in his kettle.

"Clang, clang, clink, clang." This year, the bell seemed louder and more annoying to Fred. As he walked past the bell ringer, he looked to the ground, hoping to avoid eye contact with the Salvation Army's benevolent beggar.

"Clang, clang, clink, clang." "How about a donation for the needy?" The bell ringer asked.

Maybe it was the alcohol, or maybe it was the anger, or maybe it was both, but the bell ringer's question was the spark that lit Fred's flame. Before he knew what he was doing, he grabbed the bell out of the man's hand and started ringing it as loudly as he could.

"Clang, clang, clink, clang." "You like that noise," he shouted as the poor bell ringer recoiled in fear. "You think just because you've got God on your side you can interrupt everybody else's Christmas by ringing your stupid bell?"

Then, as Fred looked straight into the bell ringer's eyes, his voice shifted into a cold, dark tone. "You bell ringers don't really care. You're just like all those other religious fanatics. You're just out for the money. Money. Money. Money. That's what Christmas is all about, isn't it? People buy Christmas like they buy cars. If you've got the cash, you can take the ride. But if the cash isn't there, neither is Christmas." And with that, he shoved the bell back at the volunteer and briskly walked away.

Over the next couple of weeks, Fred got more and more depressed as he searched for a new job. As expected, no one was hiring, and with each rejection his depression grew deeper and his drinking increased.

While Fred was out looking for work, Ginny was finalizing the family's Christmas plans. Their daughter, Lindsey, was flying in from Wichita on Christmas Eve with her husband, Rob, and their two children, Heather and Ashley. Ginny and Fred were to pick them up at the airport at three o'clock, Christmas Eve.

—w—

Around ten o'clock on Christmas Eve morning, Fred left the house telling Ginny he was going for a walk.

"Be sure to get back by noon," she reminded. "We want ours to be the first faces our grandkids see when they get into the terminal."

At eleven, Fred had not gotten back. Noon - still no Fred. Finally, at two o'clock, Ginny left for the airport without Fred.

When Fred walked out that morning, she had a feeling he would not be back in time. Now, as she wiped the tears from her face, she began working on an explanation for Fred's absence.

—w—

"Where's Grandpa, where's Grandpa?" Heather asked as she bounded through the security gate into the terminal.

Four-year-old Ashley wasn't far behind. "Where is he? Where is he? I want to see him, too," she echoed as she ran past the security guard and gave Ginny a big hug.

"Grandpa's still at home," she began, trying to convey no alarm. "He had some last minute things to do before Christmas, but I'm sure he'll be waiting on us when we get there."

The two grandchildren were disappointed but convinced. Lindsey, on the other hand, could see beyond her mother's well-rehearsed words. "Is Dad okay?" she asked out of earshot of the children.

I'm not sure," Ginny confided. "I'm just not sure at all. Ever since he lost his job, he's really been discouraged. He's drinking more and more, and there's been a night or two when he didn't get back home until the wee hours of the morning. I hope he'll be home by the time we get there, but these days, I just don't know."

The sun had begun to set by the time Ginny and her crew got back home. When Heather and Ashley got out of the car, they ran into the house yelling, "Grandpa, Grandpa, we're here, we're here."

But Fred was not there.

On the other side of town, Fred was seated at a bar, tearing off the label from his latest bottle of beer. At nine-thirty, Fred was still at the bar, the last, lone patron. At ten, Lew, the bartender began to close up so that he could go home to be with his family.

As Fred got up to leave, Lew noticed how wobbly he was and offered to take him home, but Fred declined, assuring Lew the cool air would clear his head.

Once out in the night air, Fred realized the cool air was not clearing his head, nor had his drinks erased his pain. Everything around him seemed clouded in a fog. His eyes couldn't focus on the lights. His feet seemed like his own worst enemies as he tried to walk. Soon, all he wanted to do was sleep, and for the first time in his life, Fred wished he could fall asleep and never wake up.

The steps to the storefront looked so inviting. If he could just lie down there and sleep for a few minutes he knew he'd feel better, so he staggered over to the steps and lay down.

As the light of consciousness faded away, he thought he heard a familiar sound in the distance. "Clang, clang, clink, clang. Clang - clang - clink. . . ."

Fred wasn't sure he wanted to open his eyes. If he allowed the light to seep into his head, he knew the pain would split it wide open. Perhaps he would have drifted back into that strange sleep had it not been for the aroma of hot coffee from some unknown source.

When Fred finally got his eyes open, he had no idea where he was. The last thing he remembered was falling asleep on some steps. Now he was on a clean cot, in a warm room, and several other people were sleeping on cots around him.

"Got some fresh coffee over here if you want some," a voice called out from the other side of the room.

"Where am I?" Fred moaned, almost afraid of the answer.

"You're at the Salvation Army Rescue Mission," replied the cheerful man as he poured coffee into a mug. "One of our bell ringers found you passed out on the sidewalk last night. He was afraid you'd freeze to death, so he carried you into the mission about midnight."

As reality began to peek its way through the fog, Fred wasn't sure which felt worse, his head or his guilt-stricken conscience.

After a cup of coffee and a couple pieces of toast, Fred felt better. As he looked around the mission, he saw twelve or thirteen others, all who appeared to be about as bad off as he was.

After breakfast, a young minister came to the room and invited them to listen as he shared the gospel. He read these words from John 3:16. *For God so loved the world that he gave his only begotten son that whosoever believeth on him shall not perish but have everlasting life.*

As the minister closed his Bible, he looked at the men with loving eyes and said, "Today is Christmas Day, the day we celebrate the birth of God's Son. Some will have parties. Some will eat big meals. Some will give each other very expensive gifts, but none will give a gift greater than the gift God gave to us on that first Christmas morn.

The Bible tells us that God sent his son, born in a stable, laid in a manger. God gave us the gift of his love because God gave us the gift of himself. Giving yourself to those you love is what God did on the first Christmas morning. Giving yourself to those you love is what Christmas is all about."

—⁂—

As Fred walked up the sidewalk toward his front door, he wasn't sure what he would say. How could his family ever forgive him? What could he say to his wife and his daughter to make their shame go away? What would those dear, little grandchildren think of him now?

Even before he got to the porch, the front door burst open and out ran Heather and Ashley. "Grandpa's here! Grandpa's here!" they exclaimed with unbridled joy. They looked like comic-book elves as they danced around Fred in their sleepy-feet pajamas.

The sight of such unconditional love was more than Fred could fathom. As the two loving children reached up to hug his neck, he fell to his knees and began to weep.

"Why are you crying?" asked Heather as she saw the tears streaming down his face.

"I'm just so sorry," he said. "So sorry I couldn't buy all those things you wanted for Christmas."

Quickly Ashley spoke up, "What do you mean, Grandpa? We got a lot of gifts for Christmas, and now we have the best gift of all. We've got you!"

—⁂—

For the next few minutes, Fred could do nothing but hold his granddaughters. The warmth of their love seemed to melt away the coldness of his pain.

As he took each girl by the hand and walked inside, he remembered the words of the mission preacher. "Giving yourself to those you love is what God did on the first Christmas morning. Giving yourself to those you love is what Christmas is all about."

—⁂—

Giving himself is what Fred did for the rest of Christmas Day. He played house, hide-and go-seek, and a dozen other games with Heather and Ashley. Not only did he help Ginny prepare the meal, but he insisted on cleaning the kitchen. Then, after tucking the girls into bed, Fred came down and had a serious talk with his daughter, son-in-law, and wife. He told them how powerless he had felt because he couldn't find a job. He told them how empty and angry he felt when he realized he would have no money for Christmas gifts. He told them about passing out, about being rescued by the bell-ringer, and about spending the night at the rescue mission.

"I learned a valuable lesson at that mission," said Fred. "I learned there's no greater gift we can give to those we love than the gift of ourselves."

Jeannie went over to give Fred a big hug but found herself holding back, afraid she would again be rejected. But this time Fred welcomed her affection and soon his daughter embraced him too. As they hugged him, he suddenly felt warm, much warmer than he had felt in weeks, warm as he basked in the glow of their unconditional love.

"I'll be here with you and the kids until about noon tomorrow, and then I have to go to work."

"You got a job?" asked Ginny.

"Well, yes and no," said Fred. "I've got a job but it comes with no paycheck. You see, tomorrow I'll be ringing the bell in front of the mall. Last night, the bell ringers gave so much to me; I figure the least I can do is to give back to them a part of myself.

As shoppers crowded the mall on the day after Christmas, one sound echoed out perfectly clear. "Clang, clang, clink, clang." At one time, it was the sound of Fred's defeat. "Clang, clang, clink, clang." Today, it sounded like the sound of Fred's love.

ten

It Came Upon a Midnight Drear

In him was life, and that life was the light of all men. The light shown in the darkness, but the darkness could not overcome it.
(John 1:4-5 NIV)

When Beatrice Jones marched into the office, Pastor Ivey knew somebody was in big trouble. He'd seen that face and that walk before, and whenever he saw it, he braced himself for the explosion.

"Pastor Ivey," said Beatrice, in a tone filled with hostility. "May I have a word or two with you?"

As Pastor Ivey invited her into his office, he wished a word or two was all Beatrice would share, but he knew better. Beatrice had come loaded with several words and none of them pleasant.

"Pastor," Beatrice began, "I'm sure you know I'm not inclined to complain, but when I see our church headed down the road to destruction, I feel I must say something."

As gently as he could, he replied, "Ms. Jones, what seems to be the problem?"

"You know what the problem is," she barked angrily. "The problem is that monstrous, old piano."

As Beatrice said "piano," Ivey felt his blood pressure rising. Never in his life did he imagine a church could get so bent out of shape over a piano, but "bent out of shape" was putting it mildly. The upheaval over the two pianos in the sanctuary had launched the members of Oak Grove Church into an all-out war.

—⁂—

For years, Oak Grove Church had had two pianos in its sanctuary. The large, old grand piano was situated on the right side of the choir loft and the little black spinet on the left. Though the grand piano was the better instrument, it was seldom played because it needed considerable repair. Many of its keys would stick, and when it was tuned, it would lose pitch within a week because several of its tuning pegs had worked loose.

Years earlier, the Music Committee had recommended the church spend $3,000 to refurbish the old piano, but the congregation tabled the motion until a time when the church was in better financial shape.

That's when Beatrice came to the rescue. Though Beatrice, herself, had no musical ability, her late husband, Edgar, had been the church's pianist. Just before he died, Edgar bought a new piano for their home. It was a small Wurlitzer spinet, and to be quite honest, it was an attractive piece of furniture although it was really inadequate to fill the need in Oak Grove's sanctuary.

When Beatrice learned that the church could not afford to repair the old piano, she decided to donate Edgar's new spinet to the church. Of course, an appropriate plaque was attached to the little black spinet, recognizing it as "a gift given in loving memory of Edgar Jones, church pianist 1988-2012."

Since no one knew when the church would be able to repair the old grand piano, they put the little black spinet on the left side of the choir loft while leaving the old grand piano on the right. And that's where the two pianos stayed - for over fifteen years.

Had it not been for the death of Juanita Jordan, the piano battle probably would have stayed dormant for at least another two decades; but in November, shortly after Juanita's death, her family announced that she had left $5,000 in her will to refurbish the old piano. When her daughter presented the check to the church, she said that the old piano had always been dear to Juanita because it was originally bought with money raised by the Willing Workers Sunday School Class; and, of course, everyone knew that Horatio Huxley, Juanita's father, had been President of the Willing Workers Class for over thirty-eight years.

At first, everyone in the church was pleased to learn that the old grand piano would finally be refurbished. In fact, Buster Dinsmore, down at Melodylane Music, assured the church he'd have the old grand piano back in tip top condition just in time for Christmas.

Yes, everyone was overjoyed - until - the Music Committee announced plans to move Beatrice's little black spinet to the fellowship hall; and that's when holy war broke out.

"I want to ask you something," said Beatrice as she glared into the eyes of her pastor, "I want to ask you something and I want you to tell me the truth – God knows if you're lyin.' Now tell me the truth, don't you think that ugly, old piano looks like an elephant in a doll house?"

Pastor Ivey wasn't really sure how to answer and wasn't really sure if he wanted to answer. For almost a month, he had spent the bigger part of his days listening to complaints about the two pianos. About half of the church sided with Beatrice, and a few of Beatrice's friends said they would quit giving to the church if Beatrice's spinet left the sanctuary. The other half of the church sided with the Jordan family, and several members of the Willing Workers Class threatened to leave the church and take the grand piano with them if that "tinny-soundin' little black piano" wasn't removed.

Pastor Ivey knew whatever he said would be held against him; but he'd finally had enough of the bickering, and before he realized what he was saying, he blurted out, "Beatrice, I'm gonna' tell you the truth - 'cause God knows if I'm lyin' - and the truth is this. God called me here to lead this congregation to spread the love of Jesus Christ, but instead, I've spent the last four weeks of my ministry refereeing a bunch of griping malcontents. And if you want to know the truth - 'cause God knows if I'm lyin' - I'm sick and tired of hearing about the pianos. I'm sick and tired of moderating a war over something so insignificant. Yes, I'm sick and tired of spending my days babysitting a bunch of spoiled, spiritual brats who couldn't care less about spreading the love of Jesus Christ!"

At that point, Beatrice's face turned from blush to bright red, and without another word she stomped out of the office, slamming the door behind her.

As you might imagine, it didn't take long for the news to get out. As soon as Beatrice could get to her phone, she began calling her friends, telling them how rudely she'd been treated by Pastor Ivey.

At first, those on the side of the grand piano were glad to hear that the pastor had finally put Beatrice in her place, but when word leaked out about his referring to people on both sides as "spoiled, spiritual brats," just about everybody in church got mad. And while the church couldn't agree about the pianos, they were all in agreement about Pastor Ivey. He had crossed the line and he had to go.

In Oak Grove, most of the community typically turned out for church services during the Advent Season, but this year was different. Only a handful of people attended on the first Sunday of Advent, and on the second Sunday, the crowd was even thinner.

Surprisingly, the church was almost full on the third Sunday of Advent, not because the people had a mind to worship but because, on the Saturday before, Buster Dinsmore delivered the newly-refurbished, grand piano. Though the piano looked like a custom piece of furniture and its notes rang clear and true, its music was dampened by the tension and bitterness everyone felt in the church.

It was unusually warm that fourth Sunday of Advent. All weekend the temperatures had reached into the middle sixties. Not often, but on rare occasions, Oak Grove would get a light snow by Christmas Eve, but this year, those wishing for a white Christmas expected to be disappointed.

On the week before the fourth Sunday of Advent, Pastor Ivey tried to find a family to light the Advent Candles, but everyone he asked declined. Most said they weren't coming to church. Some said they weren't ever coming back at all. So as the service started, Pastor Ivey had to light the candles himself. As he lit the fourth Candle, he reminded the few people who had gathered that the fourth candle of Advent was the Candle of Love. Then he read these words from the Gospel of John:

> *In him was life, and that life was the light of all men. The light shown in the darkness, but the darkness could not overcome the light.*

After church, Pastor Ivey went home to have lunch with his wife, Carol. For the longest time they ate without speaking a word. The past few weeks had been hard on both of them. People who had, at one time, been their best friends now refused to speak to them at all. It seemed like everybody in the community wanted them to leave, and truth be known, they were more than willing to go.

Finally, Pastor Ivey broke the silence. "Carol, I'm not sure I believe the Scripture I read today." Immediately she looked up, shocked to hear him utter such words of disbelief.

"What do you mean?" she asked.

"Well, today's text said that darkness could not overcome the light of Christ's love, but here in Oak Grove, that's exactly what has happened. This whole place is filled with the darkness of bitterness and pride, and that darkness has completely snuffed out the light of Christ's love."

On Christmas Eve day, Ivey did not go to the church. Typically, he would have spent the day making all those last minute arrangements for the Christmas Eve Candlelight Service, but since attendance had dwindled, the service had been canceled. Even if the normal crowd showed up, Pastor Ivey knew the spirit of the service would be dampened by the attitude of those who attended. He just couldn't imagine lighting candles and singing carols in a sanctuary filled with people who despised each other.

Late that afternoon, Ivey turned on his TV and looked at the Weather Channel. The meteorologist warned about a cold front moving through the area. Strong thunderstorms were predicted, possibly accompanied by high winds and hail. It looked like winter was finally coming to Oak Grove.

As the sun began to set, Ivey walked out to his porch and looked up at the clouds. They were strange-looking clouds, especially strange for the last week in December. The clouds looked mean and angry as they moved across the western sky.

Later that night the angry clouds brought the wind, then the rains. Soon, residents of Oak Grove were huddling around their TVs watching every detail of the storm warnings.

Around midnight, almost everybody heard the sound. It was loud and frightening, like the noise of an approaching train. The loudness was soon enjoined by other frightening sights and sounds. Power transformers flashed like fireworks on the Fourth of July. The crack of splitting utility poles was louder than the thunder, and the roar of angry winds was deafening.

Then there was silence - a strange silence. Nature's fury had exhausted herself, and in her wake, she left neither light nor sound.

One by one, the people of Oak Grove ventured out of their homes with candles and flashlights to assess the damage. Even in the darkness, they were shocked at what they saw. Right through the middle of town, the tornado had cut a path, a clear path where proud buildings once stood tall. Now those buildings were gone. The library was gone. The elementary school was gone, and at the end of the block, you could no longer see the steeple of Oak Grove Church. It was gone, too.

Within minutes, the stunned residents of Oak Grove began bustling into action. Neighbors started checking on other neighbors, especially those who were elderly and disabled. People with chain saws and tractors began moving large limbs off of roadways, and others helped neighbors make temporary repairs to their damaged homes.

Surprisingly, no one was badly hurt, just a few bumps and scrapes, mainly sustained in the cleanup effort. The storm's path had been a narrow one, cutting its way through a section of downtown, touching only buildings that were typically unoccupied because it was Christmas Eve.

As the residents worked on the cleanup effort, everybody seemed to gravitate to the end of the block, to the place where Oak Grove Church once stood. About an hour before dawn, 200 or so people had gathered there, sifting through the rubble to see what was left.

Beatrice Jones was there, and so were several members of the Willing Workers Class. Juanita Jordan's daughter was there, too, with coffee she had brewed on a camping stove. Juanita's grandson, Todd, started moving one of the splintered pews. As he did, his light bounced off a twisted piece of metal. When he picked it up and held it in the candlelight, he could see words engraved on it. In a whisper he read, "A gift given in loving memory of Edgar Jones, church pianist from 1988-2012."

Shyly, Todd walked over and handed the twisted piece of metal to Beatrice. When she saw it, she immediately started sobbing, and without thinking, Todd reached out to embrace her. Soon others, including members of the Willing Workers Class, came to comfort her, too.

Pastor Ivey was at the church site, standing in the area that used to be his office. As he held high his emergency lantern, he could make out pieces of his library. Books that had, at one time, stood at attention on his shelves were now nothing more than scattered pieces of rubble, almost unrecognizable with their broken bindings and shredded pages. Pieces of sermon manuscripts were scattered for blocks, and the pictures of his family that had been on his desk were nowhere to be found.

He, too, began to weep, and many heartbroken members of his congregation wept with him. Many embraced him, and those who had been so harsh to him in previous weeks offered words of heartfelt care.

Then something happened, something akin to a miracle. Beatrice's seven-year-old granddaughter, Eliza, shouted out to her grandmother. "Look Grandma," she said. "Look at all the lighted candles. This looks just like last year's Christmas Eve service at the church. When are we going to sing?"

Without prompting, Buster Dinsmore led the group in singing "Silent Night." As they sang the third verse, the words of the familiar carol took on a new meaning.

> *Silent night, holy night. Son of God, love's pure light. Radiant beams from Thy holy face, with the dawn of redeeming grace. Jesus, Lord, at Thy birth. Jesus, Lord, at Thy birth*

Yes, there amidst the rubble, "redeeming grace" dawned for the people of Oak Grove. The Son of God - love's pure light - had finally shone through the darkness.

As Pastor Ivey listened to the singing and saw his congregation reunited in love, he remembered the words of John's Gospel.

> *In him was life, and that life was the light of all men. The light shown in the darkness, but the darkness could not overcome the light.*

"No," thought Pastor Ivey, "the darkness could not overcome the light, even here at Oak Grove Church!"

eleven

The Night Christmas Came to Habeeb

"Then the King will say to those on his right, 'Come, you who are blessed by my Father; take your inheritance, the kingdom prepared for you since the creation of the world. For I was hungry and you gave me something to eat, I was thirsty and you gave me something to drink, I was a stranger and you invited me in . . .'
(Matthew 25:34-35 NIV)

Country Corners Convenience Store was all decked out for Christmas. A cardboard likeness of Santa and his reindeer stood beside the entrance. The green garland draping the gas pumps had golden bells hanging from it, and they rang like wind chimes whenever a breeze stirred. On the store's front window, Habeeb had used artificial snow to spell out the words "Merry Christmas."

Habeeb was rather proud of his decorations. Never before had he decorated for Christmas, and given his Muslim background, he wasn't quite sure how his store should look. For decorating ideas, he had taken special notice of the Christmas trappings at Jerry's Jiffy, the other convenience store in town.

"Merry Christmas," he said to himself as he admired his decorations. "Looks good, I think - looks very American. Maybe the townsfolk will see this and not harbor such hard feelings toward my family and me. Maybe, just for a time, they will forget we come from Iraq."

The last few years had been tough ones for Habeeb and his family. Habeeb and his wife moved to America in January 2001 and bought the store from one of his relatives. In those early months, business was good, but things changed drastically after the World Trade Center tragedy. Even though a decade had passed since that terrible day, many in the community still refused to do business with him because of his Mideastern heritage and his Muslim religion. That's why Habeeb made a special effort to decorate his store. "What could be more American than Christmas?" he thought. "If people see my Christmas decorations, maybe they will know I am their friend."

When Habeeb went back into the store, he opened the box containing the cheap, mail-order nativity. The characters looked strange to him. What could a drab, old donkey, a camel, and some rag-tag shepherds have in common with Santa and his elves? All the other Christmas decorations were bright and cheery, but the characters of the nativity looked so plain - and this baby in a feeding trough - what has he got to do with Christmas?

For a moment, Habeeb just stared at the characters, not really sure of their meaning, but finally he set them up on his counter, just like the ones he had seen at Jerry's Jiffy. He got them right, except for putting Joseph outside the stable with the shepherds.

Just as Habeeb got the last character into place, Zaahid burst in through the front door. Nine-year-old Zaahid was Habeeb's only child, born shortly after they had arrived in America; and though he had never lived anywhere except the United States, he still had the look and customs of a child from the Mideast.

"I hate Christmas," shouted Zaahid as he wiped angry tears from his face.

"Oh, my son, you must not say things like that," chided Habeeb. "Christmas is a happy time in America; and if we are to be good Americans, we must be happy at Christmas, too."

"Christmas is not a happy time," shouted back Zaahid. "Christmas is a time for people to hate and to hurt those they do not understand."

As Zaahid came closer, Habeeb could see that his pants were dirty and his shirt was torn. "What has happened to you, my son? Have you been in a fight?"

"You might call it a fight," replied Zaahid, "but I did none of the fighting. Some of the older boys at school caught me as I was walking home. They threw me to the ground and tried to beat me up."

"Why did they do this thing?" asked Habeeb.

"I think it started in class. At the end of the day, we had some extra time, so the teacher led the class in singing Christmas songs. Everybody in the class knew the words except me, and when the kids saw I wasn't singing, they began to point and stare. Finally, one of them passed me a note."

"What did the note say?" asked Habeeb.

"It said, 'Hey, Muslim boy. You got a problem with Christmas?' Then before I could write him back, the bell rang and the teacher dismissed us from class."

"Did you talk to this boy after class?" asked Habeeb.

"No, he and his friends left in a hurry, and I didn't see them again until I was about half way home. That's when they caught me and tried to beat me up."

As fresh tears began to run down his face, Zaahid continued, "I tried to explain about the Christmas songs, but they wouldn't listen. They just kept hitting me and calling me names. Finally, I got away from them and ran here as quickly as I could."

Lovingly, Habeeb wrapped his arms around his son and said, "Do not be afraid. You are safe with me. Look around at the store. I have placed many decorations for Christmas. When the boys at school see these things, they will understand."

But even as Habeeb uttered the words, he wondered if they were true. His family had suffered much, and he had no way of knowing just how much more suffering might come.

—◊—

After Habeeb set out his Christmas decorations, business picked up a little. Some of the town's people had been friendly to him, and a few even brought by Christmas gifts. Mrs. Crayton brought by some homemade bread, and Dr. Roberts, his next-door neighbor, gave him a bottle of homemade red wine. Habeeb thanked him but didn't have the heart to tell him that good Muslims don't drink wine.

—◊—

On Christmas Eve, most of the stores closed early. Even Jerry's Jiffy closed at six, and Habeeb was glad. If he stayed open till midnight, maybe he could replace some of the business he had lost.

From six o'clock until around nine-thirty, a steady stream of customers flowed through the store, but by ten o'clock the store was empty, except for Habeeb.

As he looked out the window, he saw an old man walking up the road toward the store. His clothes were old and dirty, and his hair had not been washed for days.

When the old man entered the store, Habeeb glanced over to the phone, making sure he knew where it was in case he had to call the police. Still, there was something disarming about the man. Granted, he had the look and smell of any other panhandler who might wander in from the street, but you could tell he was different. Perhaps, it was the warmth of his smile or the gentle look of his eyes, but within seconds, Habeeb realized the man intended no harm.

"Can I help you?" Habeeb asked.

"I hope you can," said the stranger, and as he spoke, he walked over to Habeeb's nativity. Gently he reached down and began to handle each of the figurines, one by one. Habeeb was surprised at the stranger's fascination. It was almost like he knew the characters personally. He seemed especially interested in the figurine of the Baby Jesus and handled it as though it might break. When he saw Joseph outside the stable with the shepherds, he laughed out loud and then returned the figurine to its customary position behind the manger.

Finally, he spoke. "Sir, I have no money, no food, nor a place to spend the night. When I saw your light, I thought you might be able to help me."

"I can give you something to eat," said Habeeb, "but I have no place for you to spend the night."

"That's okay, replied the old man, "My coat is warm and I can sleep on the park bench I saw downtown."

Habeeb's eyes fell on Mrs. Crayton's bread, so he opened it up and cut a large slice for the stranger. "What would you like to drink?" asked Habeeb. Immediately, the stranger eyed the homemade wine.

"If it's not too much trouble, I'd like a glass of that wine with my bread."

Since Habeeb had no other use for the wine, he pulled the cork and filled a plastic cup.

Before the stranger ate the bread, he broke it, bowed his head and whispered a prayer. He did the same before drinking the wine. Then, as the stranger ate the bread and drank the wine, he did so as though he was participating in some act of worship. While he ate the bread and drank the wine, Habeeb sensed something unusual about him. He was unlike most transients. There was something peaceful about him, something that drew you to him, something that made you want to care for him.

As Habeeb watched the bedraggled stranger eat, he thought about the way he had been mistreated by the townsfolk. In these last few years, his friends had rejected him. Faithful customers now treated him like a stranger. The boys at school had even beaten up his son. As he reflected on his rejection and his family's rejection, Habeeb realized how lonely it felt to be a complete stranger, and as he looked at the old man with his wine and bread, he realized what it must feel like to have no one who cared.

"Sir," he began, almost shocked at what he was getting ready to say. "Sir, my family's house is small, but I believe we have room for a stranger. You may spend the night at my house if you wish, and when the sun comes up, you can go on your way."

The stranger said little but simply smiled and nodded his head. In his smile, Habeeb felt a strange sense of acceptance, a warm feeling of hope, of peace, of joy, and of love.

You can imagine the family's reaction when Habeeb walked in with the stranger. Latifah, Habeeb's wife, gave him that look that only husbands can read. He knew he would hear more about this later, but he'd deal with that problem when the time came.

Within minutes, the stranger made himself at home. For some reason, he seemed especially interested in Zaahid.

"My friend," he said. "How do you like Christmas?"

Without hesitation, Zaahid barked back, "I hate Christmas and I hate Christians."

Quickly Habeeb interrupted, "My son. That's enough. I told you not to say those things about Christmas or about Christians."

"It's okay," replied the stranger. "In the last days, many will say they follow the Christ, but he will turn to them and say, 'Depart from me. I never knew you.' You see, following Jesus has nothing to do with singing Christmas carols or decorating your home. Following Christ is all about loving. So Christmas means nothing if you do not show love."

Then the stranger turned to Habeeb and said, "My friend, I know you are Muslim and that Christians have hurt you deeply. But I say unto you, you have loved me more than they. For I came to my own, but my own received me not. But you gave me bread and you gave me wine and you put a roof over my head. So behold, I bring you good tidings of great joy which shall be to all people. For unto you this day, a Savior is born, a Son is given who is Christ the Lord."

Then, without warning, the stranger disappeared right before their eyes. He did not leave the room. He just vanished. Habeeb,

Zaahid, and Latifah just looked at each other, not quite sure what to say. Something had happened, something they could not understand, but they were not frightened. Instead, each of them felt a sense of peace they could not explain.

On that next morning, Habeeb opened his store early. When he went inside, he saw that all the bread and wine was gone, and in its place was a brightly wrapped package. Quickly, he opened it, curious to see what was inside.

Inside the package he found a Bible with a brightly colored bookmark. When he opened the Bible he saw these red words underlined,

"Then the King will say to those on his right, 'Come, you who are blessed by my Father; take your inheritance, the kingdom prepared for you since the creation of the world. For I was hungry and you gave me something to eat, I was thirsty and you gave me something to drink, I was a stranger and you invited me in . . . ' (Matthew 25:34-35 NIV)

As Habeeb read the words, he began to understand what the stranger said about Christmas, and though he still wasn't sure what Santa and the reindeer had to do with the Christ, the nativity started making sense.

That was the night Christmas came to Habeeb; and after that night he was never the same.

Knowing Jerry's Jiffy would be closed on Christmas Day, Habeeb planned to take advantage of the situation by opening his store. Instead, he hung a "Closed for Christmas" sign on the front door and spent the day with his family.

For Habeeb, his late-night visitor raised more questions than answers; and while he certainly wasn't ready to discard his Muslim faith, he longed to know more about this man named Jesus, this man whose presence brought such a real sense of peace to his life.

After Habeeb and his family shared their traditional Arabic meal, Habeeb fumbled through his new book until he discovered the story of the first Christmas. He read it to his family.

When he finished reading, Habeeb closed the book and gathered his family to him, holding them tightly. There was much Habeeb did not know about the Christian faith, but one thing he knew for sure. He knew the story of Christmas, perhaps better than those who had celebrated it for years. Yes, he knew the story of Christmas, because on a cold winter's night, shrouded in the rags of a friendly transient, Christmas came to Habeeb.

twelve

So Let Your Light Shine

You are the light of the world. A town built on a hill cannot be hidden. Neither do people light a lamp and put it under a bowl. Instead they put it on its stand, and it gives light to everyone in the house. In the same way, let your light shine before others, that they may see your good deeds and glorify your Father in heaven.
(Matthew 5:14-16 NIV)

We moved into the community of Whispering Pines on the sixth day of November. For months, we searched for that perfect neighborhood, a pretty neighborhood, where people were friendly and where our kids would be safe. With its wide, clean streets and its attractive, well-kept houses, it didn't take us long to decide Whispering Pines was our perfect place.

When the moving van finally pulled away from our front door, Libby and I collapsed on the couch, exhausted from a day of carrying boxes, sorting through crates, and rearranging furniture; but it was a good exhaustion, the kind of tiredness you feel after a productive day's work.

Angie and Brad seemed to have an inexhaustible supply of energy. They had already ridden their bikes up and down the street dozens of times, and before we got our first box unpacked, they had already made friends with the kids next door.

As Libby and I sat on the couch, we started thinking about supper. Neither of us felt like cooking, so we decided to send out for pizza, but before we made the call, we heard the doorbell ring. When we answered it, we saw a pleasant looking lady standing in the doorway holding a hot casserole with insulated gloves.

"Hi, I'm Janet Justice. My husband, Rick, and I live four doors up the street, right at the corner of Spruce and Elm. We figured you folks might be getting hungry, so I decided to bring you one of my 'world-famous chicken casseroles.'"

"That's so nice of you," said Libby. "We had about decided to send out for pizza, but this'll beat pizza any day of the week. Will you stay and join us?"

"No," she said politely. "You don't need company tonight. We'll give you folks a couple of days to get settled and then maybe Rick and I can have you over for dinner."

And with that, Janet Justice said her goodbyes and headed on back to her house.

Once we had finished eating, all of us – including Brad and Angie – realized just how tired we were. So after we took baths and put clean sheets on the beds, we decided to call it a night.

Libby fell asleep as soon as her head hit the pillow, and it didn't take me long to get drowsy. As I lay there, starting to drift off to sleep, I couldn't help but notice the faint glow of light coming from somewhere up the street. At first, I thought it might be a street light, but it didn't shine steadily like street lights do. It seemed to blink off and on, off and on. The warm, white glow also seemed to reflect a faint mixture of colors: reds, blues, greens and oranges. I thought about getting up and checking it out, but I was just too tired; and before I could give it another thought, I fell fast asleep, undisturbed by the blinking glow of distant lights.

―m―

On that next morning, as we all gathered for breakfast, I asked if anyone had seen the colored lights. Brad and Angie's bedrooms were on the other side of the house, and they said they hadn't seen anything. Libby said she was so tired she hardly even remembered going to bed.

As we cleaned up breakfast dishes, Libby asked me if I would take the casserole dish back to the Justices. "Janet said they live four doors up the street, at the corner of Spruce and Elm. I bet they'll have their name on the mailbox," said Libby.

Sure enough, as I made my way up to the corner of Spruce and Elm, I saw the name "Justice" clearly etched on the mailbox. Their house was attractive, with a well-manicured lawn and two large evergreens, one on each side of their driveway.

When I rang their doorbell, a man in his middle forties answered the door. He was distinguished-looking, wearing a sport's coat and tie. His eyes were kind, and his smile was warm and inviting.

When he looked down and saw the casserole dish in my hands, he smiled and said, "I bet you're Alex Turner, aren't you? Janie said she took one of her casseroles to you guys." Then, as he extended his hand, he said, "I'm Rick Justice, Janet's husband. Thanks for bringing the dish back so quickly. I hope you folks enjoyed the meal."

"We did, indeed," I said. "Your wife's an excellent cook, and the casserole was such a thoughtful gesture. You folks have already made us feel welcomed into this community."

"Oh, you'll love this community," Rick said. "For the most part, the people here are good people. Every now and then, some of them get twisted out of shape about one thing or the other, but for the most part, they're pretty good neighbors."

"Listen, I'd love to invite you to come in and chat, but Janet and I are on our way to church. We teach the Senior Ladies Bible Study Class down at Community Church and, if we're the least bit late, those ladies let us hear about it. Perhaps, once you and your family get settled, you might like to join us at church one Sunday."

"We just might do that," I said, and then politely excused myself so that the Justices could be on their way.

—𝓶—

As I walked back out toward the road, my attention was drawn to the two large evergreens in the Justice's front yard. Though hardly noticeable,

I could see miniature Christmas lights wrapped around each tree. As I looked at the trees I remembered the lights I had seen from my bedroom window the night before. "Mystery solved!" I thought. The glowing lights must have come from the Justices' trees.

Though I didn't think much about it, I was a little surprised to see Christmas decorations up so early in November. At our house, we usually trimmed the tree and put up the lights just after Thanksgiving, but if the Justices wanted to start their celebration earlier, who was I to fault them?

Few neighborhoods are more beautiful at Christmas time than Whispering Pines. Lights, candles, wreaths and bows adorn almost everyone's home.

On Christmas Eve, the Neighborhood Association sponsors a display of community-wide luminaries. Each family places white, sand-filled lunch bags along the curb with a votive candle in each bag. When all the candles are lit, the entire community comes alive with the beauty of Christmas light. In fact, the luminaries are so impressive, people from all over town drive through our neighborhood just to see the show of lights.

By New Year's Day, about half of the Christmas decorations had been taken down in Whispering Pines, and by the middle of January, almost all the houses in the community returned to their pre-Christmas norm, but there was one notable exception.

I think I realized the exception one late night in January. When I turned out the lights and went to bed, I noticed a faint glow of light coming through my bedroom window, the same faint glow I had noticed in early November when we first moved into Whispering Pines.

"Wow," I thought, "the Justice's certainly like to make the most of the season. I guess their lights are the first to go up and the last to come down."

A week later, I noticed that the Justice's lights were still glowing. And night after night, I kept noticing the lights. They glowed in February, in March, and as the days grew longer, I noticed they still glowed after dark, even through April.

Obviously, I wasn't the only one in the neighborhood who noticed the lights. By March, the lights had become the focal point of community gossip, and by April, some of the Justices' neighbors had become visibly upset.

"People aren't going to buy a single house in Whispering Pines if those Christmas lights stay lit all year long," said Roy Randolph. "Rick and Janet are going to have to do something about those lights before they damage our property values."

Mr. Jerrod Horton, who lived next door to the Justices, was probably most angry. On numerous occasions he had cornered Rick and demanded that he take down the lights. And each time, Rick listened patiently, then responded as kindly as possible saying, "Jerrod, I'm sorry you're upset, but for reasons I cannot divulge, our lights must stay on."

By May, several neighbors tried to find legal grounds for dealing with the Justice's lights, but there was nothing prohibiting "out of season" Christmas lights in either the local zoning ordinances or the community covenant.

One night, someone sneaked onto the Justice's property and cut the wires leading to the lights. Rumor had it that it was Horton's son, Jeremy, but the lights didn't stay out long. Within a couple of hours, the Justices had repaired the damage and the lights glowed once more.

—⁂—

During the second week in May, each homeowner in Whispering Pines received a letter from Adam Renfroe, president of the Whispering Pines Homeowners' Association. The letter announced a community meeting that would take place in the fellowship hall of Community Church. The meeting would be held that following Tuesday at 7 pm, and the topic of discussion would be the Justices' Christmas lights.

On the following Tuesday night, there was standing room only in the fellowship hall at Community Church. Just about all of Whispering Pines' residents were there, and by the look on their faces, many of them were not at all happy. Of course, the Justices were there, too.

After calling the meeting to order, Adam Renfroe began. "Now, most of you know the reason we're here. We want to talk about the Justices' Christmas lights, and I figured it was only fair if we let them speak first and tell us why they didn't take their lights down in January like the rest of us."

As Rick Justice walked to the podium, you could see the concern etched on his face. Still, there was something in his eyes that made him look resolute, something firm yet caring. After clearing his throat, he spoke.

"Janet and I consider those of you in this room to be some of our best friends and dearest neighbors. In days gone by you have been there for us when we needed you, and we've tried to be there for you when you needed us. We don't just like you; we love you, and we love living in Whispering Pines.

"Now, there are a lot of things I can't tell you about our Christmas lights and a lot of things you won't understand, but I hope you'll trust Janet and me enough to be patient with us until all these things finally work themselves out.

"Please believe me when I tell you, the last thing in the world we ever wanted to do was to upset you by leaving on our Christmas lights. And if it was just a matter of making you happy, we would have taken down our lights months ago. But you see, late last October, Janet and I made a promise to God to keep our Christmas lights shining, every night, for a year. And though our decision has made some of you very unhappy, we just don't feel we can back out on our promise to God."

Even before the echo of Rick's words died in the room, Jerrod Horton stood up and in a voice that was entirely too loud said, "That's ridiculous! You're telling us that for reasons known only to you and TO GOD you've got to keep the whole neighborhood up all night with your stupid Christmas lights?"

"Jerrod," replied Rick in a much more subdued voice, "I know it sounds strange, but Janet and I are just asking you to trust us."

"Well, I'm willing to trust them," said Charlotte Kent. "Rick and Janet have always been good neighbors. Three years ago when Momma died, they were the first persons to bring food to my house; and last year when Jessie had his car wreck, it was Janet who took me to the hospital."

"Well, it's easy for you to trust them," bark Jerrod. "You live three blocks away. You don't have to put up with those blinking lights night, after night, after night. If you lived beside them, like I do, I think you'd have a little trouble swallowing all this stuff about keeping their lights on for God."

"Well, I do live close to them," said Leonard Jenkins, "and I've seen those lights blinking every night. Do I like them? Not really. Do I wish they'd take them down? I guess I do, but if they tell me they've got a good reason for keeping them on, I'm just going to trust them.

"You see, Rick and Janet have been good to me, too. They helped take care of Karen when she was suffering with cancer; and when we had to spend last summer in Houston taking care of my mother, they kept our yard up all summer long and wouldn't let me pay them a dime. I don't know why they made some kind of promise to God, but I'll just have to trust that they're doing what they believe is right."

Charlie Gray, who was the newly-appointed district attorney, spoke next in his proper courtroom voice. "Ladies and gentlemen. I don't think any of us here would impugn the character of the Justices. We all know them to be good, loving neighbors, and most of us here have been beneficiaries of their kindnesses, but this isn't just a matter of trusting someone's godly motives. This is a matter of community business. This is a matter of your property value and my property value, and every night those lights are left on, our property becomes a little less attractive.

Now, I don't know what God has told them and what they have told God, but I think they would do well to reflect on the Golden Rule and to do unto others as they would have others do unto them."

At that point in the discussion, people from all over the room began talking over each other. Some were in favor of leaving the Justices alone, and others wanted to put an end to their display of Christmas lights. Soon everybody started talking at once, and it was obvious Adam Renfroe could not restore the order.

Because everyone was caught up in the discussion, most didn't notice when Alice Bowens and her daughter entered the room. They didn't realize she was there until her wheelchair accidentally bumped into a stack of metal, folding chairs, sending them tumbling on to the tile floor.

As several of the men ran over to be sure Alice wasn't hurt, you could almost hear a collective sigh of relief when everybody realized that only the chairs had fallen and that Alice was unharmed.

But now that the attention was on Alice, the atmosphere in the room quickly changed; and as she kept moving her wheelchair toward the front of the room, no one uttered a word.

Alice Bowens was the oldest member of the Whispering Pines community. She and her husband, Henry, were the first ones to build their home in the community. It was Henry and Alice who had come up with the idea about the luminaries, and when they were healthy, Henry and Alice often put together a group of carolers to sing to those who came each year to see the community's lights.

Two years ago, Henry died, and since his death, Alice's own health had quickly deteriorated. It had been over a year since she had walked, and rarely did anyone see her leave her house except on those rare occasions when her daughter or son came to take her to the doctor.

As Alice spoke, her voice was weak, and each person strained to hear what she said. Finally, Adam lowered the microphone down to her wheelchair so that all could hear.

"As most of you know, Henry and I lived in this community long before any of you were here. In fact, we saw a lot of you grow up right before our eyes. Adam, I remember when you used to be my paper boy, and I'll never forget the day you accidently ran over our cat with your bike.

"Charlie, I remember when Henry talked you out of going to California to make your millions in the logging industry. Henry talked you into going on to college and becoming a lawyer, and look at you now. I just wish Henry was still here to see how well you've done.

"And Jerrod Horton, I remember when you were the terror of this neighborhood. People couldn't sleep at night because you and your garage band played that loud music until the wee hours of the morning. But you know what? We all knew you'd grow out of it if we'd just be patient and keep on loving you."

For a moment, Alice stopped, taking time to collect both her thoughts and her breath. Then she spoke in a voice that seemed on the verge of tears, a voice broken by the emotion of a broken heart.

"Tonight, you have come here to talk about my good neighbors, the Justices. You know they live just across the street from me, and I can see their front yard from my bedroom window. The Justices won't tell you this, but I know why they keep on shining their Christmas lights. They don't know that I know, but I do. They're keeping their lights on - because of me.

"You see, last October, when Janet came by to bring me one of her chicken casseroles, I was just about as low as a soul can be. I told her just how much I missed Henry. I told her I missed him most right after Christmas. I told her that when the Christmas lights were on, it was like Henry was here with me, but once the community became dark, it reminded me he was gone.

"Janet didn't say much at first, but then she put her hand on mine and said, 'Alice, I don't know what we can do to help, but you can be sure Rick and I will make it a matter of our prayers.'

"You see, that was what she said last October, and since that day, not a night has gone by without Christmas lights. A few minutes ago, Rick said that he and Janet had made a promise to God, a promise to let their lights shine, and as far as I'm concerned, it's not just their Christmas lights I see. I believe it's the light of Jesus Christ that keeps shining from their hearts."

And as Alice wiped her tears, everyone in the room realized the meeting was over.

These days, if you drive through Whispering Pines on Christmas Eve, you'll still see the luminaries, and chances are, you'll hear a group of carolers singing. But if you drive through here after dark on Easter or Thanksgiving or even the 4th of July; don't be surprised if you still see some Christmas lights. For in Whispering Pines, sometimes God tells people to let their lights shine, all year long, and when they do, you just can't miss the glow of Jesus shining from their hearts.

thirteen

The Gift of a Homeless Man

"In everything I did, I showed you that by this kind of hard work we must help the weak, remembering the words the Lord Jesus himself said: 'It is more blessed to give than to receive.'"
(Acts 20:35 NIV)

Devon Rigby had been standing in the cool, crisp air for almost four hours, long enough for his warm blue coat to be frosted by the glitter of new snow. It was a cold duty but one he rather enjoyed. Every Saturday in December, Devon served as a volunteer for the Salvation Army, standing by the red kettle in front of Jefferson City's Walmart, ringing his bell and wishing everyone a "Merry Christmas."

Devon helped with the Salvation Army's Christmas collection as a way of expressing his thanks. God had richly blessed him. He had a good job, a healthy and happy family and a beautiful home. He also realized that many of the people helped by the Salvation Army were not as fortunate. Most were society's rejects - hungry, homeless people who needed to know the love of Christ. In this small way, Devon felt he was doing something to share the love of Christ.

Most of the people Devon greeted were not strangers. As a local attorney, practicing in the area for more than twenty years, Devon knew almost everyone in town. But as more and more outsiders moved into the county and as children grew into adulthood, Devon was surprised at the number of faces he did not recognize.

Devon liked to watch the eyes and faces of those who placed their donations in the kettle. Some seemed excited about giving, especially the children. Happy smiles almost always accompanied their gifts. Others acted like they were fulfilling some obligatory chore by reaching into their pockets to fish out loose change.

Most people politely responded when Devon wished them a "Merry Christmas" although some would make their donation without saying a word. Some would stop and chat, and occasionally, those who were lonely would turn his casual greeting into an extended conversation.

All in all, Devon's four-hour shifts went by quickly and, at the end of the day, when he made his way back home, he always felt a sense of fulfillment, the blessing that comes to those who serve.

When Devon's four hour shift ended, he took his kettle back to Walmart's office to count the day's receipts. When he dumped the contents of his kettle out on the table, he saw the usual array of dollars, quarters, nickels, dimes and pennies. Sadly, there were always more pennies than dollars.

As Devon began to sort through the cash, a couple of bright coins caught his attention. At first glance, he mistook them for shiny pennies, but as he looked more closely, he realized they were coins he'd never before seen. Each shiny, bright coin had Lady Liberty on the front, and on the back of the coin, he saw the words "United States of America" emblazoned over four nesting eagles. At the bottom of the coin, he read, "one ounce fine gold."

Quickly, Devon got the attention of Walmart's manager and asked him to take a look at the coins. Like Devon, the manager could hardly believe his eyes.

"I don't know much about investor coins," replied the manager, "but I think these are 'American Golden Eagles'."

"How much are they worth?" asked Devon.

"I have no idea, but we can find out quickly," and as he spoke, he walked over to a corner desk and began doing a search on his computer. As the webpage loaded, the look on the manager's face relayed the message even before the words left his lips.

"If I'm reading this correctly," began the manager, "each of these coins is worth over $2,000!"

Devon couldn't believe what he was hearing. This was his eighth year of collecting donations, and his biggest single day's receipt had been $350. But today, in just two coins, he had collected over $4,000!

As Devon drove home that evening, he kept trying to figure out which of his many donors had made the lavish gift. In those four hours, he had greeted over a hundred people, and none seemed out of the ordinary.

Perhaps it was that tall businessman wearing the suit and tie. Or was it that mother who pushed the oversized stroller with twins? Maybe it was the elderly gentleman, the one who spent five minutes telling how much he missed his grandchildren who had recently moved out west. Or could it have been one of the teenagers who hurriedly dropped in his coins as he rushed off to catch up with friends? Obviously, whoever made the donation wanted to remain anonymous. Still, Devon couldn't help but wonder which of the faces he had seen that day belonged to the person making the gift.

The Sunday headline on the front page of Knoxville's *News Sentinel* announced, "Salvation Army Receives Unusual Anonymous Gifts." The lead story told not only about the gold coins given in Jefferson City but about similar donations made in Sevierville and Farragut. All in all, anonymous donors had dropped a total of ten gold coins in Salvation Army kettles across the Greater Knoxville Area, donations that raised over $20,000 for the Salvation Army's ministry.

Needless to say, the people at the Salvation Army were overjoyed by the unexpected gifts, but not for long. Along with the unexpected donations came unexpected problems.

In just two days' time, Salvation Army volunteers at two different locations were robbed at gunpoint by thieves hoping to get their hands on other gold coins. Police security was heightened, and some collection points were closed.

The Salvation Army itself also became the target of public suspicion when a local radio talk show host used the large donation as a jumping off point for his criticism of charitable organizations.

"Do we really know where all that money goes?" he asked. "Is there any public accounting for the millions of dollars collected by the bell ringers, or do the folks down at the mission spend those big bucks for anything they choose?"

Quickly, Salvation Army staffers published a statement assuring the public that its accounting was transparent and that all funding was subject to both internal and external audits. As is often the case, the talk show host had no hard facts and made his case merely by innuendo, but at days end, the innuendo raised enough questions to hamper the organization's fund raising effort.

On the following Saturday, Devon Rigby was back in front of Walmart ringing his bell. Without realizing it, he had become a local celebrity. Everyone had questions for him. What did he know? Who did he think was the donor? What did he think about the accusations made by the talk show host? Yes, everybody had questions. Sadly, on that day, the questions far outnumbered the donations.

When Devon headed back home that afternoon, he was tired and frustrated. How had something so good turned into something so dreadful? Typically, he left his task with a feeling of fulfillment, but not today. Today, the joy of service had been diminished because the true spirit of Christmas had somehow vanished behind the sparkle of twenty-four carat gold.

On Christmas Eve, the Salvation Army always invited its volunteers to have dinner with its homeless clients at their downtown shelter, and this year was no different. For Devon Rigby, it was the highlight of his holiday season, and given all the uproar about the gold-coin gifts, Devon longed to be with people who understood the true meaning of the season.

As he ate dinner with the homeless, he was reminded of the importance of his work. Eating with the homeless reminded him that he wasn't just raising money for some benevolent organization. He was helping to show the love of Jesus Christ to men and women who had lost their way.

After their meal, a local minister read aloud the Christmas story from the Bible. When he finished reading the familiar passage from Luke, he reminded his listeners that the characters in the first Christmas story were much like the people who seek refuge at Salvation Army's shelters. Mary and Joseph came to Bethlehem as homeless people, and when Jesus was born, he was born as a homeless baby.

The minister went on to say that Jesus' homeless experience caused him to love homeless people in a special way. That's why he often mentioned the homeless in his teaching and his preaching. That's why he said, "As you've done it unto one of the least of these, you've done it unto me."

After the minister finished his devotional, he invited Garrett Snyder to come and give his testimony. Garrett, a distinguished-looking man in his early fifties, maneuvered his motorized wheelchair to the microphone where he turned and faced the guests.

Devon immediately recognized him. Years ago, he had represented Mr. Snyder in a lawsuit against an insurance company. Snyder had been injured by a drunk driver and had subsequently lost the use of his legs. The insurance settlement was significant, giving Snyder enough money to care for himself and his family for the rest of his life.

As Garrett Snyder gave his testimony, he referenced his accident and described how the events of that night altered his life. In the days following the accident, he had become despondent and depressed. His permanent disability became more than he could handle. Along with his depression came a deep-seeded anger. He was filled with hate and vengeance for the man who had injured him, and he finally came to the point where he even loathed himself. With considerable emotion, Snyder told about pulling away from his family and friends and living on the streets as a homeless man.

He then related how on one Christmas Eve, he had retreated to a back alley to find shelter from the cold. While maneuvering his wheelchair through the backstreet shadows, his wheel hit a pothole and he fell over onto the street. When he tried to move, he discovered his arm was broken and found it impossible to maneuver back into his wheelchair.

After lying on the ground for several hours, another homeless man finally found him and helped him back in his chair. He pushed him to the Salvation Army's shelter where a worker took him to the emergency room and stayed with him while he received medical attention. When they left the emergency room, the worker brought him back to the shelter and took care of him for the next week.

With tears rolling down his cheeks, Snyder continued, "While at the shelter, I received more than a good meal and a warm bed. I received the love of Jesus Christ. For the first time in a long time, I was treated with dignity and respect by people who genuinely cared for me."

As Snyder finished his remarks, he looked at the shelter's director and said, "My family and I are forever indebted to the caring people of the Salvation Army. I was one of the least of these, a person who was homeless, cold, and hungry. I was one of the least of these and you ministered unto me. Your loving ministry not only saved my life and returned me to my family, but you helped me learn how to love and forgive others as I learned to love and forgive myself."

When Snyder sat down, there was not a dry eye in the house. His moving testimony was a vivid reminder to everyone present of the importance and magnitude of their work.

As the guests got up to leave, several people went over to express their appreciation to Garrett for his moving testimony. Devon, too, worked his way through the crowd, and when he finally reached Garrett, the two men embraced.

"It's been awhile since we've talked," began Garrett. "In fact, I don't think I've seen you since the trial."

"I don't think so," replied Devon. "Obviously, you're a different man than the angry one I represented eight years ago."

As Garrett turned to the woman seated next to him, he said, "Devon, you remember my wife, Angela, don't you?"

"Certainly, I do. It's so good to see you again. I'm sure you must be very proud of your husband."

"You'll never know how proud," she said as she touched Garrett gently on the hand.

"And these are our two sons," Garrett continued, motioning toward the two teenage boys seated next to their mother. "Stan is sixteen and Jason is eighteen."

"It's a pleasure to meet you, too," said Devon as he reached out to shake their hands.

Stan reached out and shook his hand firmly, but when Devon shook Jason's hand, he sensed some hesitation. For some reason, Jason seemed to be avoiding him. Instead of looking at him directly, Jason shifted his eyes to the floor, then quickly turned away, signaling that he wanted to end the encounter as soon as possible.

At first, Devon didn't think much about it, but as he looked more closely at Garrett's oldest son, he felt like he'd seen him before. This was not their first encounter. Yes, he had seen this young man before, but where?

Perhaps, he was a friend of his own son, David, but probably not. David was a student at Jefferson County High, and the Snyders lived in West Knoxville.

Had he represented the boy in juvenile court? Not likely. He certainly would have remembered representing the son of an earlier client.

Still, there was something all too familiar about the face - not only the face but about the boy's demeanor. Sometime in the past, he had seen this young man turning away from him in a way that was awkward and strained.

―⚘―

The sky was clear, and the stars shone brightly as Devon left the Salvation Army shelter and began his drive home. His experience at the homeless shelter was good for him. Once again he felt the peace, love, and joy of the Christmas season.

As he drove home, he kept thinking about his uneasy encounter with Garrett Snyder's son. Where had he seen the boy before?

Then it dawned on him. Snyder's oldest son was at the Jefferson City Walmart on the day of the gold-coin donation. He remembered the boy's awkward approach, how he turned his face away when he placed some coins into the kettle. Devon remembered saying "Merry Christmas" and getting a grunt of a reply. At the time, he didn't think much about it, but as he remembered the encounter, he realized that the boy must have been protecting his anonymity, and Devon now realized why.

All the pieces seemed to fit. The Snyders lived in West Knoxville, which begged the question, "Why would a teenager travel from West Knoxville to make a purchase at Jefferson City's Walmart?" Could it be that he was the delivery boy who had carried his father's generous donation?

Devon didn't know for sure, but it all made sense. Just earlier that evening, Snyder talked about being "indebted" to the Salvation Army. Was Garrett's $20,000 donation an anonymous payment on his debt?

—m—

As he looked at the star-filled sky, Devon began thinking back to that first Christmas night. On that night long ago, the world was changed – changed by the gift of a homeless man. Jesus Christ, born to homeless parents, quietly delivered God's precious gift of love to an unsuspecting world.

As Devon considered Garrett's generous gift, he mused at the irony. The most precious gift of the season was given by someone who had been - a homeless man.

Of course, that's not the first time that happened, is it? For what happened one day at Walmart had happened first, long ago, one night in Bethlehem.

fourteen

Nunca Solo

*The LORD himself goes before you and will be
with you; he will never leave you nor forsake you.
Do not be afraid; do not be discouraged.*

(Deuteronomy 31:8 NIV)

Without a doubt, Susan needed to be with her mother in Portland, even if it meant leaving me alone.

Gloria, Susan's mother, had not adjusted well to her father's death. Gloria was a wreck, both physically and emotionally. Before his death, Marvin had been her mainstay. He took care of the house, and all of their finances. In their retirement years, he had even done most of the cooking. Now, without her husband, Gloria was confronted with a barren landscape that, to her, was utterly frightening, a landscape of responsibility shrouded in a dark cloud of loneliness.

As the Christmas season grew closer, Susan knew her mother would need her more than ever. While holidays tend to ignite feelings of hope and joy for most people, those same festive days only exaggerate the pain and loneliness experienced by those coping with fresh grief.

Yes, Susan needed to be with her mother, and it made sense that Becky, our three-year-old, and Jana (our four-year-old) should be there, too. So we made our plan. The three of them would fly to Portland on December 1st, and I would join them the day after Christmas.

I really liked my new job at Knoxville's airport. When I went through training to be a TSA security officer, I wondered if the job might create more enemies than friends, but after a few days on the job, I discovered most people respected my position and were thankful for the safety my job helped secure.

When the work schedule was posted for December, I was not surprised to see my name on the work schedule for December 23rd, 24th, and 25th. I was the new kid on the block, and those with seniority rightly deserved the time away.

Susan and I had been married for five years, and this was the first time we'd spent the night apart. After taking Susan and the kids to catch their flight to Portland, I came back to a house that was strangely quiet. The patter of running feet and the unbridled squeals of lively, little girls had been replaced by empty house sounds, sounds that suddenly seemed so out of place. For the first time in years, I could actually hear the ticking of the clock on the kitchen wall. When the ice maker dumped a tray of ice into the refrigerator's bin, the sound almost startled me. The heating system's fan seemed much too loud, and even the house itself seemed to rebel against the silence as its timbers groaned, retreating from the winter winds that whistled outside.

Within minutes, I realized the next twenty-six days were going to be more difficult than I had first imagined. Susan and the kids were an integral part of my life, and life was certainly going to be lonely without them.

For a moment, I thought about Gloria, about the pain and loneliness she must be facing. My loneliness was real, but tolerable. My loneliness would end in a matter of days. Her loneliness would last a lifetime. In twenty-six days I'd be experiencing the hugs and kisses of my loving wife and children. Gloria, on the other hand, would have to wait for eternity.

Knoxville's McGhee Tyson Airport is not very large, but during the holidays it stays busy. As the calendar inched closer to Christmas, lines grew longer and longer at the security check point.

On top of dealing with an increased volume of passengers, we found ourselves dealing with more and more carry-on luggage. Many of the passengers brought wrapped Christmas gifts, and each of those gifts had to go through the x-ray scanner. Sadly, many gifts had to be unwrapped so that we could examine them more closely, and other gifts had to be confiscated. Unless you're a TSA officer, you just don't realize how many gifts come in liquid form, and any liquid that exceeds 3.4 ounces cannot be taken on the plane. That means we were confiscating everything from bottles of perfume to snow globes.

I really felt sorry for the well-intentioned passengers. They meant no harm. I don't know how many times I heard, "But it's only a Christmas gift," and while I hated to be the villain, I knew I could not let them travel with their prohibited items.

For a while, the increased workload at the airport was a blessing. When I was busy, I was less aware of my ever-growing loneliness. But eventually, not even the crowds could ease my pain. I missed my family. I missed them badly. Other families were celebrating the holidays, but when you're alone, there's little to celebrate.

Everything around me reminded me I was alone, and with each passing day, my loneliness became more intense. My neighbors' houses were brightly decorated. I had not bothered to put up a tree. Everyone else in the community seemed to be headed to a party, a concert, or a family gathering. I always seemed to be headed for work.

Even the airport itself reminded me I was alone. Decorative snow trees and hanging snowflakes had turned the airport into a Christmas Wonderland, and the regular appearance of Santa thrilled dozens of excited children who clamored to get a closer look; but the excited faces always belonged to someone else's children, reminding me that mine were miles away.

On more than one occasion, I'd see a mother with two small children and briefly mistake them for my own, thinking they'd come home to surprise me. Then I'd take a closer look, and reality would shatter my illusion. This was not my family. These people were the pride and joy of some other husband and father.

In better moments, I tried to take a more sensible approach. I would tell myself that many families faced much longer periods of separation and still survived. My family was simply on the other side of the country, and I would see them in a few weeks. What would I do if my family members lived on the other side of the world and I didn't see them for years?

Yes, I was being foolish, if not selfish. My mother-in-law had lost her husband and was experiencing a loneliness I couldn't even begin to imagine. My pain was nothing compared to hers. I should be proud that my family was in Portland, meeting her needs, and honestly, I was proud. Still, my sense of pride seemed little consolation for that gnawing emptiness I felt inside.

Perhaps it was a week, maybe ten days before Christmas, when I first noticed him. He was short - probably an inch or two shy of five feet. The shape of his face and color of his skin led me to surmise he was Hispanic, and the tan baseball cap he wore with Spanish words etched across the front only added to his Hispanic persona.

I knew he was part of the airport custodial staff because he was dressed in standard airport overalls, but I didn't remember having seen him before. I assumed he was one of the seasonal employees hired by the airport authority to accommodate the holiday crowds.

As he swept the floors and emptied trash cans, he did so with an unusual sense of dignity. You almost got the feeling he enjoyed being there and that this job, for him, was a blessing. In those rare moments when the crowds dwindled, you could hear him whistling softly as he worked. I did not recognize all of the tunes, but several were obviously Christmas carols.

Most people ignored him, and rarely was he greeted by an adult. Children, on the other hand, seemed drawn to him. Maybe it was his whistling, or his friendly, playful manner, but whenever children saw him, they would invariably wish him a "Merry Christmas," to which he would smile and reply, "Feliz Navidad."

On normal days, passengers are able to get through McGhee Tyson's security in less than fifteen minutes, but December 23rd was not a normal day. It seemed the harder we worked, the longer the line became. Thirty-minute waits had become the norm, and sometimes passengers stood in line for almost an hour. Despite the festive season, most travelers were not filled with peace, joy, and love. Many were angry, knowing that their last minute arrival meant they would miss their flight. Others blamed us TSA officers for their delay, suggesting we were too meticulous with our security searches. One passenger got so angry that airport security had to escort him out of the terminal.

As I helped process this throng of unhappy travelers, I found myself getting angry. Despite the crowds and the lines, these people would be spending Christmas with the ones they loved. On Christmas Day, these fathers and mothers would be rising before the break of day to watch their children excitedly open presents. On Christmas Day, these people would be having a "real" Christmas while I would be coming to a nearly empty airport to x-ray carry-on luggage and to confiscate some unhappy passenger's gift-wrapped bottle of wine.

When I came to work the next day, December 24th, I noticed the large crowd had practically disappeared. Obviously, the majority of holiday travelers had gotten to their destination, and those of us who worked for the TSA were able to process the few remaining stragglers without difficulty.

Throughout the day, I kept noticing the little Hispanic man as he cleaned up the airport. Again, he wore the cap embossed with words in Spanish – *Nunca Solo*. Not knowing Spanish, I assumed *Nunca Solo* was some Mexican resort, or perhaps the name of a popular Mexican band.

The little man seemed so pleasant, so content. His persona was immersed in an inexplicable sense of peace. Never did his work seem burdensome. Instead, he seemed to live in another world, a world where custodians were honored as highly as airport executives, a world where those being served were no greater than their servants.

Now that the crowds were small and the airport relatively quiet, I realized the little man always had a song, a song that floated so effortlessly on the wind of his hypnotic whistle; and as the notes of his carol weaved their way through my mind, I began to sense peace, a peace that had been woefully absent for the past twenty-three days.

Later that evening, I went back to the employee's lounge to take my supper break. To my surprise, the only person there was the custodian I had seen earlier in the day.

"I'm Nathan Struthers," I said. "I don't believe we've met."

"My name is Immanuel Juan José Sánchez, but my friends just call me 'Mandy.'"

"You must be new here at McGhee Tyson. I don't remember seeing you here before."

"Yes, señor. You are right. I began this job only a few days ago."

"I'm fairly new here, myself," I said. "Graduated from TSA training last July. I really like my job, but to be perfectly honest, it's been tough these last few days."

"I know," said Mandy. "I saw the crowds. You and the other officers have had your hands full."

"Yes, the last few days have certainly been toughm but for me, the toughest thing has been being separated from my family. You see, my mother-in-law lost her husband back in September, and my wife and two daughters have gone to be with her in Portland. She's really having a rough time of it, so my family went to be with her so that she would not have to face the holidays alone."

"I, too, know what it is like to miss family," replied Mandy. "My mother died several years ago, and I live with my father. I have never taken a wife, but my father and I have provided a home for many children, especially those who are orphans. We cannot stand the thought of these children going through life alone, so we have adopted them into our family. In fact, that is why I am here. I've been sending money back home to my father so that he can give gifts to all our children on Christmas Day. I will not be able to see their happy eyes as they open their gifts, but I will be happy just knowing I have helped make them happy."

As Mandy spoke, I began to realize just how selfish I had been. Instead of focusing on my mother-in-law's needs, I had spent the entire Christmas season bemoaning my own misery. Granted, I was lonely, probably lonelier than I had ever been, but there was a positive side to my loneliness. By giving up what was precious to me, I had helped a dear lady who had lost what was precious to her.

—m—

At 11 pm my shift ended, and I went to the employees' parking lot to get my car. As I walked toward my car, I noticed I had left the dome light on. As I saw it glowing faintly, I suspected that it was a foreshadowing of trouble to come.

Just as I had suspected, my car wouldn't start. Seemingly, the battery was dead. I tried to start it several more times without success.

Just as I had given up hope, I heard a knocking at my window. There stood Mandy with a pair of jumper cables in his hands.

"Maybe I can help," he said, and within a few minutes, with Mandy's help I was able to start my car.

"Thank you so much," I said as Mandy rolled up his cables and put them back in his old truck. "Can I give you something for your trouble?" I asked.

"No trouble at all," he said. "I was glad to help."

As I began to pull out of my parking space, Mandy came back to my car. "Sir," he said. "I was just thinking. This is Christmas Eve. You are without your family. I am without my family. No one should be alone on Christmas Eve. I am headed to my church to celebrate Christmas Eve midnight mass. Most of the people there will be Hispanic, but they will make you feel like family if you will join us on this special night?"

"But I'm not Catholic," I said, half-heartedly looking for an excuse to decline Mandy's invitation.

"You don't have to be Catholic," said Mandy. "I know the priest very well, and he will treat you like family."

Never, in all my life, did I imagine spending Christmas Eve celebrating mass with a group of Hispanic Christians, but for some reason, Mandy's invitation seemed impossible to decline, so I consented to go.

Midnight mass at the Iglesia Del Nino was an experience I will never forget. Mandy was right. As soon as I walked into the church, I was made to feel like family. Before I knew it, I was being embraced by men, women, boys, and girls who could barely speak my language.

When the service began, I felt the presence of God in a way I had never felt before. Surprisingly, my lack of Spanish didn't seem to matter. There was a spirit in the church that transcended language, a spirit of peace, love, and joy, a spirit of celebration for the birth of God's King.

When the priest invited members of the congregation to come forward to take communion, I hesitated.

"Come," whispered Mandy. "Come with me and celebrate the body and blood of Christ."

"I'm not sure I should," I whispered. "Remember, I'm not Catholic."

Then, with a smile that dismissed all my fears, Mandy assured, "It will be fine. Remember, I know the priest, and he will be glad to see you come."

So I followed Mandy to the altar and watched him as the priest dipped the communion wafer in the wine and place it on his tongue. When Mandy stood to leave, I took his place and knelt where he had knelt.

Words cannot explain what I felt as the communion wafer touched my tongue. Quite unexpectedly, I sensed a presence that can only be explained by the word "divine." And though my family was miles away, I no longer felt alone. I was a part of a family. Brothers and sisters were by my side, and though we didn't even know each other's names or speak each other's language, we all felt connected, connected by a Spirit that embodied us all.

The room was lit only by candlelight, so I had a little difficulty finding my way back to my seat. At first, I thought I had moved into the wrong row because I could not see Mandy: then I looked at the seat beside me. There it was, Mandy's tan baseball camp etched with the words "Nunca Solo."

When the service was over, I tried to find Mandy, but he was nowhere to be found. When I asked others if they had seen him, most did not understand my question, and the few who knew English simply said that Mandy had disappeared. By that, I assumed he had simply left.

On Christmas Day, as I expected, the airport was virtually empty. Employees easily outnumbered the few passengers who made their way to the gates.

I looked for Mandy, but he was not there. Maybe he had gotten the day off. With his hat in my hand, I went to find the custodial supervisor.

"Mandy left his hat at church last night, and I thought you might return it to him when he comes back to work."

A puzzled look crept across the supervisor's face. "Mandy?" he asked. "I have no custodian named Mandy."

"I'm sorry," I said with a chuckle. "His real name is Immanuel Sánchez. Mandy's just a nickname.

"Sorry, but I have no employee named Immanuel Sánchez," he said. "Are you sure he was a custodian here at McGhee Tyson?"

"I'm sure of it," I said. "Surely you remember him. He's the one who whistled Christmas carols as he worked."

At that, the supervisor broke into laughter. "He did what? Whistled Christmas carols as he worked? Are you sure you've not been dipping into the eggnog a wee bit early?"

—m—

It was late afternoon on December 26th as my flight touched down in Portland. Even before I saw them, I heard their voices.

"Daddy. Daddy. Daddy." I saw them running down the hallway toward me, and they looked like angels in all their glory. Jana got there first, followed by Becky. Susan and her mother were several steps behind. For the longest time, we barely said a word. Hugs and kisses were language enough.

As we started to walk toward baggage claim, Susan stopped and just stared at me.

"What is it, I asked?"

"Where did you get that cap?" she asked in a voice that reflected more incredulity than curiosity.

"It's a long story, an amazing story," I said.

"I'm sure it is," replied Susan. "You see, this is not the first time today I've seen that cap."

"What do you mean," I asked.

"Just before we headed to the airport, we stopped at the mall to exchange some gifts. When we came out, our car wouldn't start. Almost out of nowhere, a short, little man came out to help us. He looked Hispanic, must have been an inch or two short of five feet.

"At first I was cautious, but as he spoke, I could tell he simply wanted to help. He was such a pleasant man. When he opened the hood and started working on the car, I couldn't believe my ears. He was whistling, whistling Christmas carols as he worked. Soon he had our car running again. As we left, the kids wished him a Merry Christmas, and he replied with 'Feliz Navidad.'

"Now here's the crazy part. He wore a cap, a tan cap just like the one you're wearing, a cap embroidered with two Spanish Words – *Nunca Solo*.

"*Nunca Solo*." It took me a few seconds to remember my college Spanish, but soon the words made sense. *Nunca Solo* means 'never alone.'"

Never alone – that's the message at the heart of the Christmas story. Why else would God give his Son the name Immanuel? Christmas means, "God with us." We are never alone. He's there in our times of loss, there in our times of loneliness, and there in the dark night of our soul. He's there so we are never alone.

The Gospel writer Matthew said it well. *"Now all this took place to fulfill what was spoken by the Lord through the prophet: "Behold, the virgin shall be with child and shall bear a son, and they shall call his name Immanuel," which translate means, "God with us."*

Immanuel. God with us. *Nunca Solo*. We are never alone.

fifteen

The Light that Darkness Could Not Extinguish

In the beginning was the Word, and the Word was with God, and the Word was God. He was in the beginning with God. All things came into being through him, and without him not one thing came into being. What has come into being in him was life, and the life was the light of all people. The light shines in the darkness, and the darkness did not overcome the light."
(John 1:1-5 NIV)

The winter Wyoming sun disappeared quickly behind the mountains surrounding the little town of Paxton; and as darkness crept over the city, one house after the other began to glow with the warmth of holiday lights. At the Engelmann's house, Rachael and her little sister, Rebecca, had already begun to argue.

"It's my turn tonight," said Rebecca. "You got to light the candles last night."

"So. . ." taunted Rachael, "I'm the oldest, so I should light more candles than you; besides, the last time Father let you light the candles, you lit the wrong ones."

"Did not."

"Did, too."

"Did, not."

"Wait a minute, wait a minute," interrupted their mother as she emerged from the kitchen. "There are eight nights of candle lighting, so each of you gets to light the candles on four nights; and if I'm not mistaken, Rachael, you got to light the candles last night, so it's your sister's turn tonight."

Just then, the girls heard the garage door opening.

"Daddy's here," said Rebecca. "I wonder if he brought us a present tonight."

"Of course, he did," chided Rachael. "It's Hanukah and we get presents on every night of Hanukah."

"I know," said Rebecca, "that's why my friend Candice wishes she was Jewish. Christians only get presents on one day. We get presents on every night of Hanukah."

"I'm home," roared the deep voice of Joel Engelmann, and at the sound of his voice, both girls rushed to the door to greet him with a big hug.

"Are those latkes I smell frying in the kitchen?" ask Joel.

"They sure are," said Hannah, his wife, "and I'm glad you didn't work late. There's nothing I hate more than having to reheat latkes after they've gotten cold."

These fried potato pancakes, called latkes, were a favorite of the Engelmann family, and no one in Paxton fried them up better than Hannah Engelmann. During Hanukah, she often served them with beef or lamb, and for dessert, she made her own jelly-filled donuts from a secret recipe passed down from her great-grandmother who still lived in Jerusalem.

"Do you have a present for us?" asked Rebecca.

"A present?" teased her father. "Why should I have a present for you on this night?"

"Because it's the sixth night of Hanukah," said Rebecca, "and we get presents on every night of Hanukah."

"There will be plenty of time for presents," replied her father, "but first we must light the candles and say our Hanukah prayer. So come on, girls. Let's all go into the dining room and get the evening started."

There weren't many Jewish families in Paxton, but during Hanukah it was easy to tell where the Jewish families lived because each family had a Menorah displayed in the front window of their home. The Menorah is a special candle stand with four candles on each side and one tall candle in the middle. The tall candle is lit first, and then it's used to light the candles on each side. On each night of Hanukah, a new candle is lit until, on the eighth night, all the candles are lighted.

As the Engelmanns gathered in the dining room, the father lit the center candle of the Menorah and then gave it to Rebecca, who lit three candles on the left side and three candles on the right.

"I'm glad she got it right this time," whispered Rachael to her mother who greeted her words with a disapproving stare.

"Who will tell the story of Hanukah tonight?" Joel asked.

"I will," said Rachael, "I know every word of it by heart."

"I know it, too," exclaimed Rebecca.

"Do not," said Rachael.

"Do too," said Rebecca.

"Okay, okay! That's enough out of the two of you," chided Hannah. "If I hear anymore arguing from either one of you, there will be no Hanukah gifts tonight. Now, Rachael, go ahead and tell us the Hanukah story."

At that, Rachael stood, as if making a grand presentation to a crowd of thousands, and in a theatrical voice, she said, "Many years ago, when our ancestors were slaves to the Syrian King, the Jewish people were very sad. They were sad because the evil king would not allow them to worship God in His Holy Temple. Instead, the evil king brought dirty animals into the Temple and made sacrifices to false gods.

"When God saw the evil things done by the Syrian king, he spoke to Matthias, a Jewish priest, and told him to fight against the Syrians so that the Jewish people could once again be free. So Matthias and his five sons gathered all the Jews together, and they revolted against the Syrian king; and by the strong of arm of God, they won freedom for all the Jewish people."

Then Rachael's voice got very soft as she told the next part of the story.

"In the temple, there was a sacred lamp called the Menorah, and it always burned to remind the people that God was with them. On the day of Jewish freedom, the priest came to the temple to light the Menorah, but when he looked at the lamp, he realized there was only oil enough to last one day.

"'What shall we do?' cried out the people. 'It will take eight days to get more oil. How can we keep the lamp of God burning if we have no oil?'

"Quickly the priest quieted the people and said, 'Fear not, for if God can free us from the Syrians, surely he will make a way to keep his lamp burning.'

"And so the priest lit the Menorah, and the lamp burned all day and all night - not for just one day, not for just two days - but the lamp burned for eight days and eight nights until the priest could get more oil.

"'It's a miracle, cried out the priest.

"'It's a miracle,' replied the people.

"And so from that day on, Jewish people everywhere have celebrated Hanukah by lighting candles for eight days so that they can remember the miracle of God in his Holy Temple."

When Rachael finished the Hanukah story, she took a bow, and the family applauded her telling of the story.

"Hannah, will you lead our Hanukah prayer tonight?" asked Joel.

"Of course, I will," said Hannah, and at that, each member of the family bowed their head and closed their eyes.

As Hannah held her hands toward the heavens, she recited the ancient prayer,

"We light these lights for the miracles and the wonders, for the redemption and the battles you made for our forefathers, in those days at this season, through your holy priests. During all eight days of Hanukah these lights are sacred, and we are not permitted to make ordinary use of them except to look at them to express thanks and praise to your great Name, for your miracles, your wonders and your salvation."

Then all four family members said in unison, "Amen."

It happened in that brief silence that followed the Amen. Without warning, the sound of shattering glass broke the silence as a large rock exploded through their dining room window.

"Get out of here, Jew!" cried a voice filled with ugliness and hate. "Get out of here, Jew. Don't you know this is Christmas and we don't need no candle-lightin' Jews stealin' our American holiday." And as the tires screeched, the carload of vandals sped away, yelling obscenities as they disappeared into the night.

At first, the family sat there in shock. A second or two later, the girls began to cry. Rachel's arm had been cut by flying glass and the plate full of latkes lay on the floor, its shatter pieces mingled with fragments from the broken window. The Menorah also lay on the floor with most of its candles broken.

Quickly, Hannah went to Rachael and began to tend to the cut on her arm. "You'll be okay," she said in a reassuring voice. "It's not a deep cut. Here. Let's go into the kitchen and I'll clean it up and put a Band-Aid on it."

Rebecca had run to the safety of her father's arms, sobbing as he held her closely. "What happened, Daddy?" she asked. "Why did those people break our window and say those terrible things?"

"I'm not sure," said her father, although he was surer than he admitted. This was not his first taste of anti-Semitic violence, and he feared it would not be his last.

"Hannah," he called into the kitchen. "I'm going to start cleaning up this mess. Why don't you call the sheriff and tell him what happened."

Minutes later, Sheriff McKenzie was at their front door. Joel Engelmann welcomed him into the house and immediately took him to the dining room to show him the broken window.

"I'm so sorry this happened to you folks," said the sheriff. "Was anybody hurt?"

"Rachel got a little cut on her arm, but nothing serious," he said. "I think the girls are more afraid than hurt."

For the next few minutes, the sheriff listened carefully and took notes as the family detailed the events. Then, after spending several minutes examining the crime scene, he pulled Joel Engelmann aside.

"Can we go somewhere and talk alone," he said.

"Of course," said Mr. Engelmann. "Why don't we go into my study?"

Once in the study, the two men sat down and the sheriff began the conversation. "Joel," he began with a sound of concern in his voice. "I'm afraid your house is not the only house that's been hit this week. Last night, two other Jewish homes were vandalized. The night before, three Jewish homes were attacked. Each incident was the same. These vandals evidently pinpointed Jewish homes by looking for the Menorah in the window. In every case, the vandals struck just after the family had lighted their Menorah."

For a moment Sheriff McKenzie paused as his face grew even more serious.

"Joel, I'm going to be honest with you. I don't think this is just a case of teenage vandalism. I think we're dealing with a hate crime. As you know, most of your neighbors here in Paxton are good, loving, law-abiding Christians. That's why you can see Christmas decorations from one end of town to the other. But there are a few bigoted people in town who just don't like Jews, and when they see your lighted Menorah, they think you're belittling Christmas. Now, it's a free country, and I'm not going to tell you what to do, but I think for your own safety and for the safety of your family, I'd take your Menorah down until Christmas is over."

At first, Joel Engelmann sat quietly, not sure how to respond. Then, with words that were chosen as carefully as they were spoken, he replied,

"Sheriff McKenzie, I thank you for your concern and for your care, but we will not be removing the Menorah. The Menorah is a symbol of our faith. It reminds us that God is always with us, not only in good times but also in times of trouble. If I removed the Menorah, it would say to my daughters that these hateful people are stronger than God. No, we will light our Menorah on all eight nights of Hanukah and trust our lives to God. Hanukah is a remembrance of the miracle God performed many years ago. Who knows, maybe God will do another miracle today."

On the next day's edition of *The Paxton Herald*, the headline read, "Vandals Victimize Jewish Homes." The story detailed the rampage of violence that had swept across Paxton, violence that appeared to be aimed at Jewish families who were celebrating Hanukah.

When the people of Paxton read the news story, many rushed to the defense of their Jewish neighbors. Before the morning was over, people from all over town had come to offer their help and support to the Engelmanns. Some brought food, and others brought tools to help repair the broken window.

Everybody in town began talking about the violence aimed at their Jewish neighbors and friends. The violence had left an ugly mark on the entire town, and the people of Paxton expressed their collective outrage.

For years, Jewish families had lived peaceably in Paxton. Their children had gone to public schools, and except during religious holidays, you couldn't tell the Jewish children from any of the other children.

Granted, Christmas time was a bit awkward. Sometimes carolers would accidently come to the door of a Jewish home and greet the family with Christmas carols. And while the Jews could have been offended, they chose to greet the carolers with a smile and sometimes offered them jelly-filled donuts. When the carolers sang, the Jews would try to hum along even though they didn't know the words to these Christian hymns.

To be quite honest, it wasn't always easy to tell which house was Jewish and which was Christian because all the houses were decorated with lights. Of course, only the Jewish houses were decorated with Menorahs.

I think it was Rev. Jamison, pastor of St. Joseph's Church, who decided that something needed to be done to stop the senseless violence. That's why, on December 23rd, he called a meeting of concerned citizens to see if there was something they could do. The meeting would take place in the church's fellowship hall.

People from all over town attended the meeting, but the Jewish families were conspicuously absent. While they appreciated their neighbors' concern, they felt strange about being the focus of community attention, and so they chose to stay at home and let the Christians do what they thought was best.

The meeting at St. Joseph's lasted several hours, and there seemed to be a special magic in the air when everyone walked out of the fellowship hall. Nobody said anything, but you could tell by the look on their faces that something good was about to happen.

The last day of Hanukah coincided with Christmas Eve, and as the Engelmanns prepared to light their Menorah, they wondered what the night would bring. Would they be able to celebrate this last holy night in peace, or would the vandals return with their words of hate and their acts of violence?

Just about the time Hannah finished preparing their Hanukah meal, the girls once again heard the garage door open.

"Daddy's here," yelled Rebecca, and both girls rushed to the door to see if he had brought them gifts.

Joel's face had a strange look on it as he walked into the house. "Hannah, Rebecca, Rachael," he yelled out. "Grab your coats and come quickly. We must go outside."

"What's outside? What's outside?" asked Rachael and Rebecca.

"I can't tell you. It's a surprise. You'll just have to come and see for yourself."

Quickly, all three of them grabbed their coats and burst through the front door. As they looked up and down the street, at first, nothing seemed unusual. Every house on the street glowed with holiday lights, and the town of Paxton looked like a magical fairyland as large, white snowflakes began to fall.

"Where is it?" asked Rebecca. "I don't see anything."

"I see it. I see it." cried out Rachael, her voice bursting with excitement.

"I see it, too," yelled Hannah, hardly believing her eyes.

"I still don't see it," said Rebecca. "Somebody show me the big surprise."

At that, her father picked her up and said, "Rebecca, look at the front windows of everybody's house and tell me what you see."

Carefully, she scanned the front window of every house on the street, and then in a voice that was loud enough to be heard all over town, she cried out, "I see it. I see it, too. God has done a miracle, just like he did on the very first Hanukah."

Perhaps it wasn't a miracle, but if not, it was the next best thing. Every house on the street had nine candles lit in the front window, one tall candle in the middle and four smaller candles on each side.

Not only was this true on the Engelmann's street; it was true all over town. Every house in Paxton glowed with the light of nine candles, and for one blessed night, it was impossible to tell the difference between a Jewish home and a Christian home because every home glowed with the light of God's miraculous love.

—m—

And so on Christmas Eve, there were no acts of vandalism in Paxton. The vandals had no way of knowing which homes were Jewish and which ones were Christian because the light in everyone's home overcame the darkness that had invaded their town.

That year, the attendance at St. Joseph's Christmas Eve Service was larger than ever, perhaps because there were some new faces in the crowd. And while some of the worshippers sang those familiar carols of "peace on earth good will toward men," others just hummed along because they did not know the words. Yes, they did not know the words, but on that night in Paxton, Wyoming, everyone knew their meaning.

And as all the worshippers held their candles high in the air, Rev. Jamison ended the service with these words from the Gospel of John:

In him was life, and the life was the light of all people. The light shines in the darkness, and the darkness could not overcome the light.

About the Author

For over twelve years, Gene Wilder has served as Senior Pastor of The First Baptist Church of Jefferson City, Tennessee. While being regularly published in newsletters, newspapers, and magazines, this is his first book.

In 1990, he was honored with the "Golden Pen Award" from Macon News, Macon, Georgia. In 1994, one of his sermons was published in Best Sermons 7, Harper Collins Publishers, and in 1998 and 1999, he was awarded "First Place, Serious Column in a Weekly Paper" by The Georgia Press Association.

Gene, and his wife, Pat, have two adult children, and three beautiful granddaughters, who provide all the inspiration any author could require. Gene's hobbies include travel, golf, music, drama, and hiking.

You may contact the author at: gene@gene-wilder.com, or you may learn more about him and his work at: www.gene-wilder.com.

Made in the USA
Monee, IL
09 August 2024

63449248R00075